A Note to Readers

While the Morgan family and their relatives are fictional, the events they find themselves in are real. In 1896, more than ten thousand Minneapolis schoolchildren helped move the Stevens house to Minnehaha Park. Almost one hundred years later, in 1983, children re-created the event and moved the house again.

A more serious problem that faced Americans in the 1890s is still with us: alcohol abuse. "Drunkards," as alcoholics were then called, often lost their jobs and beat their families. Women who had seen the terrible things alcohol could cause formed the Women's Christian Temperance Union, or WCTU. They worked to educate people about the dangers of alcohol and pass laws that would make the sale of alcohol illegal. In later years, they also worked to reform prisons, gain women the right to vote, and end child labor.

A BETTER BICYCLE

Norma Jean Lutz

BARBOUR
PUBLISHING, INC.
Uhrichsville, Ohio

To Dr. Timothy T. Tregoning—for keeping me fit for long hours at the computer. Thanks!

ISBN 1-57748-292-1

Published by Barbour Publishing, Inc.
P.O. Box 719
Uhrichsville, Ohio 44683
http://www.barbourbooks.com

Member of the
Evangelical Christian
Publishers Association

Printed in the United States of America.

Cover illustration by Peter Pagano.
Inside illustrations by Adam Wallenta.

CHAPTER 1

The Shady Vinewood Club

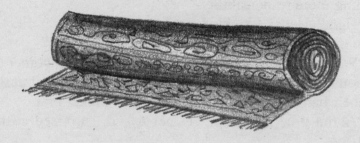

Spring had exploded in the Fair Oaks neighborhood of Minneapolis. Pussy willows were out in the park and japonicas were blooming their fiery red.

Eleven-year-old Peter Morgan was aching to go enjoy the beautiful Saturday, but he was being held captive against his will. He put all his anger and frustration into another swing of the rug beater. Dust flew out of the heavy Persian rug that hung over the back clothesline.

"Gee whitakers, Peter. How much longer?" Peter's best friend, Heber Meeks, stood leaning against a nearby tree. "I thought you said we'd spend the whole day at the club-house."

"Watch your language. Mama'll hear you and tell your mama." Peter slammed the rug beater again and again. "This is the last rug." He stopped and gave a gigantic sneeze, then slammed the rug again.

"Our girl does all the cleaning at our house," Heber said, shifting from one pudgy leg to the other.

"I know," Peter said, "but Mama says we can't expect Stella to do everything." This rug, the largest and heaviest of all, made Peter's arms ache to slam it so hard. He glanced over at Heber. "And Mama also says I'm supposed to be learning more responsibility."

"Ugh." Heber wrinkled up his nose. "I never like it when my parents start talking about responsibility."

"Well, it's about time," came a voice from the corner of the house. Peter looked around to see his sister Carol pushing their baby brother Mark in the white wicker pram.

"About time for what?" Heber asked, surprised at the intrusion.

"About time for Peter to learn responsibility." Even though Carol was two years younger than Peter, she liked to talk as though she were older. "I'm the one who has to do all the work around here," she added.

Suddenly, six-year-old Allyson came bounding out of nowhere and began to dance circles around the pram. She sang a little song to herself and fluttered the fringe on the pram's parasol. Her antics made her baby brother giggle.

"If I have to watch the little ones," Carol went on, "why should Peter get to go have a day of fun?"

Heber shot a worried look in Peter's direction. But Peter just shook his head to assure him there was no need for concern.

Giving the rug one last smack, Peter said to Heber, "Help me carry this in the house. Then I'll be ready to go."

For all Carol's fussing, Peter knew she wouldn't make any trouble. She was a pretty good sister as sister's went.

Heber huffed and puffed as he took one end of the rug and helped Peter carry it around to the front porch of the house.

"We'll roll it up and leave it in the front hall," Peter told him as he held the front screen door open with his foot.

"Then will we get on over to the vacant lot? Avery's gonna wonder where we are."

"Avery can come this direction if he's worried. He could ride over here on his fancy new bicycle."

Avery Norton was the third member of their trio. He lived further into the heart of Fair Oaks, where the sloping lawns were larger and every home had a carriage house in back. The fact that Avery was the owner of a new bicycle hadn't set well with Peter. It didn't seem fair. After all, Avery wouldn't turn twelve until a month after Peter. Why should he get a bicycle first?

Peter guessed it was because Avery was the baby of his family. And because of the fact that the Nortons had plenty of money. Avery's father owned a flour mill right next to the Pillsbury mill over on the Mississippi River, and they were very rich.

"I need to make a stop at the toolshed before we go," Peter explained as they struggled to roll up the rug.

"Seems to me we should just scat," Heber replied.

"Peter? Is that you?" Stella called from the parlor.

"It's me and Heber," Peter answered.

Stella appeared at the door of the front parlor with a

large feather duster in her hand. Her maid's apron, which that morning had been starched and spotless white, was now wrinkled and soiled.

"Oh good," she said. "Hello, Heber. Since both of you are here, I want you to pull the rug into the parlor and spread it out for me. I've just finished mopping the floor." She turned and went down the hall.

As fast as they could, the boys dragged the rug from the hallway into the parlor. Once the rolled-up rug was situated at one end of the room, they unrolled it and left it lying at a cockeyed slant.

"Hurry," Peter whispered. "Out the door." He led the way around the porch, down the side steps, and around the opposite side of the house from where Carol was playing with Mark and Allyson.

"What do you need from the toolshed?" Heber asked, puffing along a few steps behind Peter. "Can't we just get while the getting's good?"

"We need paint and brushes. I asked Father last evening for permission to take them."

"Oh yeah. For our signs."

"That's right." Peter lifted the latch on the wooden toolshed. Inside was dim and cool. The air was full of earthy aromas mixed with odors of paint and turpentine. Here was where Mama kept all her flower pots and Father kept his tools. "Up there, Heber." Peter pointed to a shelf on the far side. "Grab three paintbrushes. I'll get the paint."

In a matter of moments, Peter had latched the toolshed door, and they were headed down Vine Place toward the vacant lot on Shady Lane. The vacant lot was halfway between Avery's house and the block where Heber and

Peter lived. Heber's house was five houses down Vine Place from Peter's.

Sure enough, Avery was sitting in the doorway of their clubhouse, with his shiny red bicycle leaning against the trunk of the great oak tree nearby. Avery had all the good looks of the three, with his dark wavy hair and his long straight nose. He jumped to his feet when he saw them coming. "Where've you two been? I was about ready to hop on my bicycle and come and find you."

"Peter was busy learning responsibility," Heber said with a chuckle.

"Never mind," Peter said, "we're here now, and we brought paint and brushes."

"Look here." Avery pointed behind the clubhouse. "Your uncle Abe brought by some tar paper. He said if we nailed it on the roof, it'd keep the rain out."

Peter smiled. Uncle Abe was really swell! "We'll paint the signs first," he said, "then we'll work on the roof."

"We need to have a club meeting first," Avery told them.

"Oh sure," Heber agreed. "A club meeting." He looked at Peter. "We need to have a club meeting since we're a club."

Avery's father belonged to a lodge, a men's club downtown, and the country club at the edge of town, so it had been Avery's idea that they create a club of their own. He waved toward the door of the clubhouse, inviting them inside. They ducked their heads as they went in.

There wasn't much in the clubhouse just yet. After all, it had only been built a few weeks earlier. First they had had an old wooden crate to play in. Even though it was small and cramped, it made a great place to play. That's what had given them the idea to build a real clubhouse.

After that, they made several trips to the lumberyards near the river for scraps and had built the little house all by themselves. Well, almost by themselves. Heber's sixteen-year-old brother, Martin, helped some. The clubhouse was the shape of a small lean-to with one window in the front and one in the back. The windows were just open squares with wooden shutters and no glass.

Heber's mama had given them a few carpet scraps to put on the ground. And it was Peter's idea to lay castoff newspapers under the carpeting to keep out the dampness.

Since the club had been Avery's idea, he appointed himself president. Now he sat cross-legged on the carpet and said, "I call this club meeting to order." Since he didn't have a real gavel, he used a stick, which he tapped against the wall. "The first order of business is to name our club."

"A name," Heber said. "What a good idea. We need a name."

"And since," Avery went on, "our clubhouse is on Shady Lane, and since you two live on Vine Place and I live on Ridgewood Avenue, I think the name should be a mixture of the street names. Something like The Shady Ridgewood Vine Club. What do you think?"

Heber nodded, but Peter shook his head. "That's too long. I like Shady Vinewood Club better," Peter said. "It's easier to say."

Heber looked at the two of them. Peter could tell he wasn't sure where to put his vote. Heber was often caught between the two of them. But Avery settled it by saying, "You know, Peter, I think you're right. I like that much better. The Shady Vinewood Club it is!"

"What do you think, Heber?" Peter asked.

Heber nodded. "I like that just fine. Now let's paint signs and fix the roof. It could rain anytime, and we don't want our carpets to get wet, do we?"

Outside, Peter took a stick and pried the lid off the can of black paint. They had saved extra boards to use for their signs. "One board will have our name," Peter said.

"And the other will say, 'No girls allowed,'" Avery added. "That'll be one of the first laws of the club—absolutely no girls!"

"Agreed," Heber said with a smile.

"Agreed," Peter said, although he really wouldn't mind if Carol were allowed to come in sometimes. After all, Carol was nothing like Avery's bossy older sister, Naomi. Fifteen-year-old Naomi bossed everyone—even children other than her brother.

"Be careful not to flick any paint on my new bicycle," Avery told them.

Peter wished Avery wouldn't keep referring to the bicycle. Peter wanted to pretend it wasn't even there. But how could he, when the April sunshine was glinting off the bright red metal and the steel handlebars?

The sunshine was warm, so Peter took off his jacket and put in on the ground beside him. As he carefully painted the sign, he kept looking over at the bicycle and for the millionth time wished he had one like it. Except the one he wanted was royal blue. He'd seen it sitting in the window of Holmgren's Bicycle Shop just down Hennepin Avenue from Grandpa Enoch's bank.

Peter made up his mind. Tonight at supper, he would again ask Father if he could have his very own bicycle. Of course he knew he could never receive one for no reason at all, as Avery had. But at least he could ask for one for his birthday. But his birthday was in September—way after summer was over. And September seemed years and years away.

"Hey, Peter," Heber said, "look at your suit."

Peter looked down at his pin-striped sailor suit. There were drips of black paint on the front.

"Oh no." Peter sat back on his heels. He looked at his two pals, whose clothes were also splattered with paint. If Mama saw this, Peter might never get a bicycle.

CHAPTER 2

A Boy in Overalls

The tar paper was in place, and the signs had been hammered into place on the sides of the clubhouse. The signs had a few drips and a few smears, but otherwise they looked fine. The boys were sitting inside resting from their labors as Avery read a chapter from his newest dime novel. It felt deliciously wicked to have a place where they could read the forbidden books without getting into trouble. At least they were forbidden to Peter and Heber.

Avery was lucky. His parents didn't care one way or the other about the novels. That's why Avery could go to the drugstore and walk right up to the book and magazine counter and purchase a dime novel and never get into any trouble at all.

Not only did Peter's parents speak out against the books, but also Grandpa Enoch. "It's a frightful waste of time to fill your head with empty nonsense," Grandpa would say in his gravelly old voice. "Stay your mind on the classics, my boy. They give rigorous exercise to the brain!"

Search for the Silver City was the title emblazoned on the cover, and Avery was at the most exciting part. Budd Boy and his friends were about to uncover the treasure in an old mining town when Dangerous Dan got the drop on them.

All of a sudden, Heber said, "Look there!"

Peter jumped, and Avery dropped the book. "Don't do that, Heber," Avery said.

"No, look." Heber pointed out the small window. "Someone's out there. By your bicycle."

"My bicycle!" Avery pushed Heber out of the way. "Hey you! Yeah, you there. Get away from what doesn't belong to you."

Peter had crawled over to the window and was peering over Avery's shoulder. It was a boy. A boy who looked to be about their age or perhaps a little older. But he was wearing overalls. Overalls and a plaid flannel shirt. No one in Fair Oaks wore overalls.

"I saw him first," Heber said under his breath. "Let me see." He pushed Peter back from the window, but not before Peter saw a very sad look pass over the boy's face.

"Aw, I wasn't touching your dumb old bicycle," Peter heard the boy shout back.

"Is he going?" Peter asked.

Heber nodded. "He's leaving."

"He'll leave if he knows what's good for him. I'll lick him good," Avery said as he picked up the book and found his place. "What do you make of that?"

Heber's eyes were wide in his round face. "What a funny way to dress. Do you suppose he's visiting somebody around here?"

"He'd have to be," Avery put in. "No one looks like that who lives in Fair Oaks." Then he added with a laugh, "Maybe we should make a second rule: No one dressed in overalls allowed." The thought of that sign made them all roar with laughter.

Later they played with their tin-can telephones. One would stay inside the clubhouse, another would go outside, and they would talk on the cans attached with string. They played they were important businessmen making million-dollar deals. Soon the tall trees cast long skinny shadows across the vacant lot, telling the boys suppertime was near. That and their growling stomachs.

"It's getting late," Peter told them. "We'd better be getting home."

"We need to bring food next time," Heber complained, rubbing his pudgy midsection. Heber was nearly always hungry.

"We'll bring food all right," Avery said. "And I have just the thing to keep it in."

"What thing to keep what in?" Heber asked.

"I have something to keep food in. You'll see. I'll bring it over tomorrow."

"Aw shucks," Heber said as he went out the door. "You know my mama won't let me out to play on Sunday afternoons."

15

Peter grabbed up the paintbrushes and the can. "I'll tell her you won't be playing. We'll just be sitting in the clubhouse."

"You'd do that?"

"Sure. You'll go with me, won't you, Avery?"

Avery gave a nod as he gingerly lifted his bicycle from where it rested against the oak tree. "Yeah, Heber. Count on us. Peter and me'll get you sprung from prison."

They laughed at his joke. Peter watched for a moment as Avery rode off on his bicycle, then turned to walk with Heber back to Vine Place.

"Do you think Avery will ever let us ride?" Heber wanted to know. He took a couple quick steps to catch up with Peter's long-legged stride.

"Sure he will, Heber. Soon's the new is worn off, he'll be insisting we take turns on it."

"I sure hope the new wears off fast." He hurried his steps as they turned onto Vine Place. "And I hope I'm not late for supper."

"You're not." Peter pointed to the girls playing hopscotch on the sidewalk in front of the Meeks's house. Carol and Heber's sister Odele were the same age and were as close friends as Heber and Peter.

"If Odele is still out playing, you're safe," Peter told him.

Carol was hopping effortlessly through the series of squares drawn on the sidewalk. The ribbons hanging down from her straw sailor hat and her long black pigtails bounced with every jump.

"Thank heavens," Heber said with a sigh.

All the houses in Peter's neighborhood looked nearly alike—two-story homes with wraparound front porches and touches of ornate wooden trim on the porches and around the eaves. Some had trim white picket fences around the front yards. Although the houses were not as large as the ones where Avery lived, Peter was quite content with his house on Vine Place.

"Hey," Heber called out to the girls. "You'll never guess what we saw."

"Everything you looked at," Odele quickly replied, which sent the girls into fits of giggles. Odele's auburn hair lay in long ringlets down her back and over her shoulders. She flipped the curls back as she laughed.

Carol's dark eyes lit up with merriment. Her smile had a way of lighting up her entire face. Peter often heard people say the two of them favored one another, but he knew his face was not as open or bright as Carol's. At first glance one might think it was Heber and Carol who were siblings since Carol was more on the plump side and Odele was lanky and thin.

Heber didn't much appreciate their joking. His mind was still on the boy in the vacant lot. Peter kept thinking about him, too.

"Be serious," Heber said. He picked up the stone from the hopscotch square where his sister was now ready to scoop it up.

"All right," she said. "We give up. What did you see?"

"There was a boy in the vacant lot who was dressed like he'd just come off the farm. He had on overalls and a flannel shirt. He was touching Avery's bicycle, but we shouted at him and he ran off."

Carol and Odele glanced at one another. Peter saw it, but he didn't think Heber did.

"Actually," Peter put in, "the boy didn't even touch the bicycle, Avery was the only one who shouted at him, and the boy walked off—he didn't run."

"That's what I said," Heber protested. "Well, almost that's what I said." He turned back to the girls. "You know of anybody around here who has country cousins visiting?"

Odele took back the stone from Heber's hand, replaced it on the seventh square, and started again from the first. After finishing a flawless leap from square to square and neatly picking up the stone while balanced on one foot, she looked over at Carol. "Are you thinking what I'm thinking?"

Carol nodded.

"What is it?" Heber said. "Do you know something about the boy?"

"A family moved in over on Prospect Street this afternoon," Carol said. "Odele and I saw the moving wagon drive by, so we followed."

"They didn't have much to unload," Odele said. "Not much at all."

"So what does that have to do with the boy?" Heber said in a huff.

"The family's name is Dawes," Odele told him. "We met the girl, whose name is Mathilda. Mattie for short. She told us she has a brother named Harry."

Heber's eyes grew wide. "You don't mean it. You think that boy could be him? The boy named Harry? You suppose he *lives* here?"

Carol shrugged. "Could be."

Just then, Mrs. Meeks opened their front door and stepped onto the porch. "Heber! Odele! Come wash up. Supper's ready."

"Coming," Heber answered. Turning back to the girls, he asked, "This Mattie, was she dressed like you?"

Both Carol and Odele had on ruffled lawn dresses with big puffed sleeves and fussy sashes. Their high-topped button shoes and long white stockings were immaculate and their hair bows straight, in spite of the fact that they'd been playing outside most of the afternoon. Carol and Odele looked at one another again.

"Well?" Heber said, inching toward the house.

"Was she?" Peter echoed.

"Not exactly," Odele said.

"Come on, Peter," Carol said, grabbing at his arm. "We'd better get home."

Heber stepped up on his front porch and called back to Peter. "We'll get to the bottom of this tomorrow."

Down the street, Peter saw Father step off the electric trolley and disappear into the house. Then he could hear Mama calling to them to come to supper as the nearly empty trolley went clanging on down the street, depositing passengers who were coming home from work.

"You're right, Heber," Peter said. "We'll find out what's going on." He and Carol fell into step as they went on up the sidewalk toward home. "What did you mean, Carol? Tell me more about Mathilda Dawes."

"You can see her for yourself soon enough. Mattie's a nice girl. I'm sure they're fine people. And besides, what's so bad about overalls?"

A shrill ringing from up the street interrupted their talk.

"It's Aunt Elise!" Carol said with a squeal.

Their aunt was riding her bicycle back home from downtown. Uncle Abe and Aunt Elise lived in a sprawling house near Avery's. She waved to them and called out, "Hello, children." Then she rang the bell on the handlebars one more time.

They called back to her and watched as she steered the bicycle over to the side of the street and stopped, resting her foot against the curb. Aunt Elise was the only woman in all of Fair Oaks who rode a bicycle. And the only one Peter knew of who wore a bicycle suit with her skirt length barely down to her calves. Grandpa Enoch said it was a disgrace! But Peter and Carol both thought Aunt Elise was daring and delightful.

"Isn't it a glorious day?" she said to them, quite out of breath. She straightened her jaunty cap, which was similar in fashion to Peter's corduroy one.

"Yes, glorious," Carol agreed. "Especially if you have a bicycle to ride anywhere you want."

Aunt Elise laughed and patted the handlebar. "It does give one a modicum of freedom, my dear."

"Where have you been," Peter wanted to know. "Just out riding?"

"Oh my, no. I've been at the mission down near the riverfront. Several of the WCTU ladies have agreed to help out there as much as we can."

Peter knew that WCTU stood for Women's Christian Temperance Union and that those brave women extended mercy to the drunkards who hung around the saloons. It was a scary place down on skid row. There were many able-bodied men who were afraid to go there.

Aunt Elise shook her head at the thought of her day's work. "The poor souls are trapped and enslaved by demon rum. But we've seen a few set free by the power of our merciful loving God." She smiled. "It makes all the hours of work worthwhile! Excuse me now, children, I must be off. Your uncle Abe is waiting for me."

With that she gave a little shove, wobbled a moment, and then went peddling smoothly and easily down the street.

"Do you think it's terribly hard to learn?" Carol asked softly.

"Learn what? To ride a bicycle?"

She nodded.

"Naw. I think it would be easy to learn. Avery sure learned fast."

"I don't see what keeps it upright. It looks so. . .so precarious."

"And so adventuresome!" Peter added with a note of wistfulness in his voice.

"Maybe you could learn to ride on Aunt Elise's bicycle," Carol suggested.

Peter gave her a withering look. "That's a woman's bicycle. Besides, I know Avery is going to let both Heber and me learn on his."

Carol gave a shrug. "Somehow Avery doesn't seem to be a sharing type of fellow."

"You just don't know him very well."

He followed Carol up onto their front porch. She turned to look at him. "Don't you think you'd better take those things to the toolshed?" She pointed to the paint and the brushes in his hands. "And change your suit before dinner?"

"Oh yeah." How could he have forgotten?

CHAPTER 3
Spies

Peter was able to make his way in the back door, through the sunporch, and up the back stairs. He then pulled a clean suit from the tall wardrobe in his room and changed clothes before going down to supper. Father was a stickler about all the children being clean and in their best bib-and-tucker for the evening meal. Tomorrow he'd try to get the suit to Stella. She'd get the paint out for him.

Peter stood before the mirror at the washstand and carefully parted and combed his dark hair with a wet comb to make every wisp lay in place. If he was going to approach Father about the bicycle again, he wanted to look his best.

He firmed up his garters and straightened his long stockings, making sure his knee pants were creased and neat, then headed for the stairs.

Before he was halfway down the stairs, sounds of Mark's pitiful wailing met his ears. Supper was ready, the food was on the table in the dining room, but everyone was in the kitchen hovering around Mark. Carol and Allyson stood by the kitchen door.

"What's happening?" Peter asked.

"Mark's finger got caught in the swinging door," Allyson said, her little pixie face looking sad.

Peter winced. No wonder the toddler was wailing so.

"I'm so sorry, ma'am," Stella was saying over and over. "So very sorry. I just didn't see him at my heels as I came through the door."

Father was chipping a piece of ice from the block in the icebox with the ice pick. "It's all right, Stella," he said gently. "We know you aren't negligent with the children."

Mama, who was cradling Mark in her lap, said to Father, "Now you see what I mean, don't you, James? We truly do need another girl. All the cooking and cleaning is just too much for Stella. She can't possibly do all that and watch the children as well."

Father took the cloth handed to him by Stella and created a little ice pack with it. He knelt by Mama's chair and put the ice on Mark's wounded finger. The child's wailing had subsided to whimpering, but when Father touched it with the ice, he began to cry again. Peter could see the finger was turning a nasty purple.

"There, there, Mark, old man," Father said, "the ice is going to make the pain go away." Father's voice was kind and soothing. Peter used to love to have Father come to his bed-side when he was sick. Just the sound of Father's gentle voice had a way of making everything all better. Within moments, Mark was quiet except for a few hiccupping sniffles.

"I'll take him to his bed," Mama said as Father helped her to her feet.

Stella came forward. "Let me, ma'am. You tend to your dinner. Everything's ready."

Mama nodded her agreement. Mark's eyelids were growing heavy. Gently Stella took Mark from Mama's arms and carried him up the back stairway.

"Come everyone," Father said herding his little flock out of the kitchen into the dining room. "Let's eat before everything turns cold."

Father had changed from his Prince Albert suit to his dark velvet jacket with the silk sash. He took his place at the head of the table, where he proceeded to take the Bible from the sideboard and read a passage of Scripture. This he did every evening. Sometimes the children would say their memory verses as well. Carol was by far the best at memo-rizing Scripture. Peter usually stumbled through his.

After returning thanks, Father carved the juicy pot roast. Mama dished up the vegetables, and plates were passed to the children. When everyone had started eating, Mama said, "Now, James, about hiring another girl." Peter had to give Mama credit for her gentle persistence.

"Polly," Father answered, "fitting the salary of another domestic into our budget at this time isn't feasible. With four hungry children to feed, it's taking all we can spare just to pay the present expenses." He smiled at Mama. "Remember, I'm just an officer in your father's bank, not the owner."

"I wish you were the owner," Allyson chimed in. "Then you could go into the big vault and give us money whenever we wanted some. Wouldn't you, Father?"

"Father can't do that," Carol corrected her. "Not even Grandpa Enoch or Uncle Abe can take money whenever they want."

"Then why do Grandpa and Uncle Abe have bigger houses and more servants than we do?" Allyson demanded, making a little pout with her lower lip.

Father had to chuckle at this remark. "That's easy to answer. Your grandfather has been amassing his funds for a great deal longer than your mother and I have. And as for your uncle Abe and aunt Elise, they haven't any little mouths to feed, nor little bodies to clothe."

Mama reached over to pat Allyson. "Much to their loss. You children are worth more than all the money in the world."

Allyson smiled.

Peter had only been half listening. Part of his mind was thinking about the strange boy named Harry. The other part of his mind was dreaming of the royal blue bicycle parked inside the toolshed—sitting ready for him to ride at a moment's notice.

"Father," Peter said when the conversation had died down a little, "Avery has his own bicycle, and I was wondering if I could have one as well. There's a royal blue one in the window of Holmgren's Bicycle Shop downtown that would be perfect."

Father glanced at Mama, then back at Peter. "Son," he said, "have you not heard what I was just saying about the state of our finances?"

"Oh, I didn't mean right away, although I wish with all

25

my heart it could be right away. I was thinking perhaps for my birthday. That's five whole months away. That would give plenty of time for the money to become available."

Father smiled. "And what makes you think our financial situation would have changed in the next five months? Do you know something that I don't know?"

Peter knew Father was joking, but Peter didn't want to joke. The subject was too serious.

When Peter didn't answer, Father said, "Tell me, what's the price of this coveted vehicle in the shop window?"

"Twenty-nine dollars," Peter answered.

"Twenty-nine dollars," Father repeated. "Is it trimmed in pure gold?"

The look of surprise on Father's face made Peter wish he'd chosen one of the cheaper models that were kept inside the store, rather than displayed prominently in the window. Of course twenty-nine dollars wasn't much to Avery's father. But then Avery's father owned an entire flour mill.

"Your request has been heard," Father said to Peter. "All I can say at this point is, we'll see."

"Thank you." Peter knew Father was always fair with him. Even though the amount seemed large, Father would at least consider it.

Mama spoke up then. "You might speak to Grandpa Enoch about the matter, James."

Father helped himself to another slice of roast beef. "That's a thought, Polly. I may just do that."

Peter didn't see how that would help anything. Grandpa Enoch was hopelessly old-fashioned. But Peter kept silent. It was kind of Mama to think of it. At least neither Father nor Mama had given him a flat-out no.

"A new family moved in on Prospect Street today," Allyson said when the conversation lulled. "But they don't have much furniture, and there aren't any children my age."

"Perhaps all of their furniture hasn't arrived," Mama suggested. "That happens when people move long distances."

"Maybe," Allyson agreed, "but it all came in a moving van."

"How curious," Mama said.

"I met the girl," Carol put in. "Odele and I introduced ourselves."

"How neighborly of you," Father commended her. "What's the family name?"

"Dawes. The girl's name is Mathilda. She said to call her Mattie. She didn't seem very happy."

"Moving can be difficult," Mama said, "especially for children. Perhaps she's had to give up friends. But with you and Odele around, she won't be sad for long."

Peter couldn't imagine having to move away from Fair Oaks. He'd been born right in this very house, and he knew every square inch of the neighborhood all the way from Park Avenue to Lyndale Avenue, and that included Central Park with beautiful Johnson Lake situated like a diamond in the center. All the places that were so familiar to him would be strange and new to the boy in overalls. Peter again thought of the sad look he'd seen on the boy's face.

Stella came in then with one of her rich cream pies. "Markie is fast asleep," she told them as she set the dessert plates and the pie at Mama's elbow.

"Thank you, Stella dear," Mama said. "Even if we can't afford to hire more help around here, I want you to know you're worth a dozen just like you."

Young Stella blushed a bright pink. "Thank you, ma'am," she said softly.

After supper, Heber came over, and he and Peter played catch in the backyard. When they tired of that, Heber suggested they go around the block to Prospect Street and see if they could get a look at the new family.

Peter gave the ball a toss in the air and caught it. "Why? Why would we want to go and just look?"

"We could be the spies and learn the truth about the boy in overalls, then report back to Avery tomorrow."

"That is, if your mama will let you play."

"You said you'd help me get out," Heber reminded him. "How about it? Are you coming or not?"

Peter put the ball away on the sunporch at the rear of the house. "Lead the way."

Although lights were on in the house on Prospect Street, heavy draperies were drawn. Peter felt a little silly spying out a house just a block away, but Heber said, "We'll tell Avery we tried. We can report all we know to him tomorrow."

"But we don't know anything yet," Peter protested.

"We know more than he does." That seemed to be important to Heber.

When they arrived back at Peter's house, Heber waved good-bye. "See you at church tomorrow," he called out.

"See you."

Peter turned to go inside. In a way he was glad they couldn't see anything at the Daweses' house. It was one thing to pretend to spy. It was quite another to actually spy on real people. It seemed like snooping. He also found himself hoping that the boy in overalls had nothing to do with the Dawes family.

28

CHAPTER 4

The Password

On Sunday morning, Avery and Heber were already in their seats in their Sunday school classroom in the basement of the church when Peter arrived. Peter was late because Mark had pitched a fit when Mama tried to bandage his hurt finger. It made the whole family late.

Mrs. Chenoweth, their teacher, had already marked the roll and had started the lesson. She was teaching on the Good Samaritan. Peter was embarrassed to have to interrupt. The open area was filled with wooden folding chairs, but there was no seat beside Avery and Heber. He had to sit with Carol across the room from his friends. Allyson went into one of the side rooms with the younger children.

Avery had a way of making the other kids giggle while Mrs. Chenoweth was trying to teach. He could wiggle his ears and make funny faces without her seeing him. Mrs. Chenoweth was a good teacher, but she wasn't as strict as their fifth grade teacher at school, Miss Minor. If Avery acted up at school, Miss Minor could cart him off to the principal's office.

Peter found himself giggling along with the rest in spite of himself. But he also heard the Bible story that Mrs. Chenoweth was telling about the man from Samaria who took time to stop and help a hated Jewish man. No one else would stop, not even the religious leaders. Mrs. Chenoweth made the story very real. Her large hat covered with flowers and birds and a loose veil sat forward on her high pompadour. The flowers bounced as she told the story.

Peter wondered about that man who just happened along. How interesting it would be to meet that Samaritan man and talk to him. What was it that made the man so bold? Why would he take the time to stop when no one else cared? Did he forget that Samaritans and Jews were supposed to hate one another?

Peter wished he could ask Mrs. Chenoweth his questions, but he would be embarrassed in front of Avery and Heber. That didn't stop him from wondering.

When the bell rang and they filed upstairs into the sanctuary, Heber said to Peter, "I wonder if Martin will be able to get Naomi's attention today?"

"It'll be fun to watch and find out," Peter answered.

"I think you're mean," Carol said from behind them. "It's not fair to laugh at them just because they're sweet on one another."

Avery, who was close by, said, "What do you mean *they?* Poor old Martin's advances don't seem to be received or returned." Then he snickered, and they laughed along with him.

"Poor old Martin," Heber repeated.

"Yeah, poor, poor old Martin," Peter chimed in.

Even though the boys weren't allowed to sit with one another in the sanctuary, they were able to crane about and exchange looks. It was great sport to watch as Martin attempted to gain the attention of the very pretty Naomi and failed miserably. At times, it was all the three boys could do to smother their giggles. Peter didn't hear much of the sermon.

After church, the Morgans rode to Grandpa Enoch's house in his large brougham. Every week they ate Sunday dinner with Grandma and Grandpa. Grandpa's house was just down the street and around the corner from Aunt Elise and Uncle Abe's, who always came to dinner as well. Even though the seats faced one another in the large open carriage, it was still a bit snug with all six of the Morgans. Mark was fidgety and fussy, and Mama had to keep shushing him. Peter would have liked to have sat up with Grandpa's driver, but that was not allowed.

Grandma Tina was a wizened little lady with pure white hair piled high on her head and crowned with a fashionable little hat filled with spring flowers. She gave an understanding smile to Mark and reached across to pat his little hand. Grandma's hands were almost transparent, with many blue veins rising up. To Peter, she looked frail as a porcelain doll.

While Grandma was gentle and quiet, Grandpa was

blustery and loud. Mama often told the children not to be upset by Grandpa's roar. "His bark is worse than his bite," she would say. Now he scowled at Mama and said, "What's the matter with that boy? Doesn't he like to go to church?"

Patiently, Mama explained about Mark's hurt finger and added that he needed a nap.

Grandpa huffed a little at that, making his thick white mustache quiver, and tapped his cane impatiently on the side of the carriage. Peter also knew that often Grandpa Enoch was in pain. He lost a leg while fighting in the War Between the States, and he walked with a wooden leg. Father explained that Grandpa's joints were getting stiff, and that the wooden leg was often very painful where it attached to Grandpa's body. "Instead of complaining," Father told Peter and Carol one day, "he just snaps at people. Even me."

"Does he snap at Uncle Abe?" Peter had asked.

Father just laughed. "Yes, but nothing much bothers your uncle."

Today Grandpa seemed to be in one of his more gruff moods. When they pulled to a stop in front of their large stone house, Grandpa's driver hopped down and opened the doors of the carriage to assist the passengers. When it came Grandpa's turn, he pushed the man's hand away and said, "When I can't get out of my own carriage under my own steam, I'll be the first to let you know." With that he firmed his black top hat, braced himself against the door of the carriage, and hoisted himself up and out.

"Now, now Enoch," Peter heard Grandma say gently. "Jager was only trying to help. He's doing what you hired him to do."

Inside, the front hall was filled with the aromas of baked ham. Grandma's cook had prepared a scrumptious ham dinner, and all was spread on the table in the large front dining room.

Everything at Grandpa's house always seemed so much bigger and rather stiff and formal, but the arrival of Uncle Abe and Aunt Elise made it less so. Uncle Abe, who had a ready laugh and ready wit, was always cutting up and making Peter laugh. Mama always said her brother Abe was still a boy at heart.

During dinner, Grandpa brought up the subject of the WCTU, saying how he felt women should stay at home and mind their families.

Aunt Elise was not moved one whit by his remarks. She continued eating with a smile on her face. To see her in her azure church dress with lacy puffy sleeves, a high collar pinned with a jeweled brooch, and her sweeping skirt and proper bustle, no one would ever imagine she was the same woman who had donned a daring bicycle suit a day earlier.

When Grandpa began to talk about the impropriety of women riding bicycles, Peter knew for certain his grandpa was hopelessly old-fashioned.

"It's a disgrace, that's what it is," Grandpa spouted, "for a lady of refinement to be peddling about the city on such a contraption."

Still Aunt Elise did not react. Presently Father changed the subject to banking, and Grandpa forgot about scolding Aunt Elise.

Peter was relieved when a dessert of rice pudding with raisins was served. He never liked to hear Grandpa say unkind things about Aunt Elise or her work. As soon as he was finished, he asked Mama if he could be excused. Avery would be by any minute.

"Where will you be going, Peter?" Mama asked.

"Avery's coming for me. We're going to our clubhouse."

Hearing his remark, Uncle Abe asked, "How did the tar paper work out?"

"Swell," Peter told him. "Thanks for your help."

"I don't think you should be playing in your Sunday clothes," Mama said.

"I won't get dirty. We'll be sitting inside on the carpet pieces Heber's mother gave us."

"Well. . . ," Mama said.

"Come on, Sis," Uncle Abe said. "What can it hurt? Don't you remember what it was like to be a child?"

"Please, Abe," Mama said with a smile. "You're not being much help."

Just then, Grandpa cleared his throat and wiped his white mustache with his napkin. "You there, Peter. Come here, young man."

"Me?" Peter asked, which made Carol and Allyson both giggle.

"I do believe you're the only Peter in the room. Come here."

Grandpa seldom addressed Peter directly. The boy stepped to the head of the table, and Grandpa pushed back his captain's chair. "I've been told you want to own one of those newfangled vehicles called a bicycle."

"Yes, sir," Peter said firmly. "I do want one very much."

Grandpa smoothed his mustache. "Be in my office at the bank next Saturday morning at nine o'clock sharp. You and I will talk about this matter man to man."

Peter felt his heart skip a beat. What a surprise that Grandpa would even consider talking about it. "Yes, sir, I'll be there." Turning to Mama, he said, "May I be excused now?"

Mama nodded. "Be home by five."

"Yes, ma'am."

With both Avery and Peter speaking on Heber's behalf, Mrs. Meeks agreed to let him go with them to the clubhouse. Once the three of them were together, Avery said he had a surprise to show them. This news quickened their steps all the way to Shady Lane. Peter stepped inside, and there against one wall he saw a small hand-carved wooden chest.

Heber followed right behind Peter. "My goodness, Avery," he said in a low voice. "Where'd you get such a swell chest?" He went over to touch it.

Avery looked quite proud of himself. "In our attic. Father said I could have it. Or rather, that *we* could have it. It's for all three of us." He pulled something from the pocket of his knee pants. "And look here," he said. There in his hand lay three small brass keys.

"A key for each one of us?" Heber's eyes were wide.

"I had our man, Franklin, go to the hardware store yesterday and have these made. But I didn't want to show you the chest until I had the keys."

"It's a good surprise, Avery," Peter told him. And Carol had said she didn't believe Avery could share. A lot she knew.

Avery fit one of the keys into the lock and turned it. He lifted the lid. Inside lay a stack of six dime novels, a package of salt crackers, and two tins of sardines. It was just the

35

right size for them to store the things they needed for the clubhouse.

"Food!" Heber said peering inside.

"We can keep all our special secret things in here," Avery told them. "And now men, hold out your right hands." Peter and Heber stretched out their right hands, and into each upturned palm Avery placed a key.

Avery then clasped the remaining key, making a tight fist, and placed his fist on the chest. "Put your hand holding the key on the chest," he instructed. Solemnly the other two boys placed their fists on the smooth top of the wooden chest.

"The holder of the key to the chest is a fully ordained member of the Shady Vinewood Club," Avery pronounced. "As president of the club, I hereby deem that Heber Meeks, Peter Morgan, and Avery Norton are all full-fledged and accepted members of the club."

"Hurrah," Heber said.

"All for one and one for all," Peter said.

"Friends to the end," Avery said.

"May I try my key?" Heber asked.

"Be my guest." Avery moved away from in front of the chest so that Heber could get to it. Heber locked and unlocked the chest not once, but three times. He seemed fascinated with it.

"What about a password?" Peter asked. "Shouldn't a club have a secret password?"

"Good idea," Avery replied. "Any suggestions?"

As Heber opened the chest one more time, Peter glanced at the cover of the novel *Search for the Silver City*. "How about 'Budd Boy?' "

"Splendid idea!" Heber said. "Budd Boy is our hero!"

"Budd Boy it is," Avery agreed. "From now on, whenever we approach the clubhouse, members are required to use the password."

Avery pulled *Search for the Silver City* from the chest and picked up reading where he'd left off the day before. Avery had a wonderful way of putting life into the stories. Peter was sure Avery would make a great dramatic stage star.

The boys were kept breathless as Budd Boy was tied with ropes inside the cavernous mine shaft. Dangerous Dan had lit the fuse on the dynamite. Budd Boy was sure to be blown to smithereens.

"Ooh, I'd beat the dickens out of that Dan fellow," Heber said.

"Don't interrupt," Avery said. With great cunning, Budd Boy dragged himself to a sharp rock and used it to cut the ropes. He was able to stop the burning fuse just in time. Then he snuck out of the cave and captured Dangerous Dan. It was a wonderful ending.

"We'd better get on home," Peter said as Avery closed the book. "I bet it's nearly five."

Avery pulled out his silver pocket watch with the engraving of a stag deer on one side. Snapping it open, he said, "Fifteen minutes till."

The watch was new, and Peter had forgotten Avery had it until he pulled it out. It seemed Avery had most everything. "Thanks," Peter told him as he stood to go. "Come on, Hebe, your mama will be looking for you as well."

The spring warmth of the afternoon was quickly vanishing. A cold north wind had whipped up, and gray clouds were gathering. None of the boys had worn jackets.

"Brrr," Avery said as he hopped on his bicycle. "Feels like winter's coming back again."

"Thanks for the swell chest," Heber said. "See you at school tomorrow."

"See you," he called back as he rode off.

Peter and Heber talked excitedly about the club all the way back to Vine Place. The brisk cold wind hurried them along. At the Meeks's house, Peter bade good-bye to Heber, then hurried on down the street. A glimpse through the houses to the next block made him stop in his tracks. There was the boy in overalls. And he was barefooted!

CHAPTER 5

Grandpa Enoch's Proposition

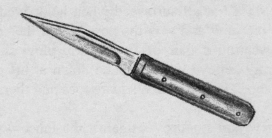

Peter hadn't planned to spy, but his curiosity compelled him. He moved through a neighboring yard and into the alley, keeping himself well hidden behind the fences. At a break in the fence, he peered through. Peter could hardly believe the boy was wearing no shoes. His feet must be chunks of ice, but he wasn't hurrying like a chilled person would. Perhaps he was used to being cold.

Peter continued to slip between houses and behind fences until he saw what he wanted to see. The boy went up the stairs and onto the porch of the house on Prospect Street. The one that Carol had said the new family moved into. The barefoot boy opened the front door and went inside. Peter gave a loud sigh. That meant the boy must be Harry Dawes.

Avery's parents had not yet given him permission to ride his new bicycle to school. Not because they didn't trust him, but because they were concerned that the other children might scratch it up or damage it. So on school days, Avery walked to Heber's house, the two of them walked to Peter's house, and then the three of them walked the eight blocks to Fair Oaks Elementary School.

Carol and Odele were either behind or ahead of them—usually behind because they liked to talk and giggle and dawdle.

Peter wasn't at all surprised when he arrived at school that next morning and saw the new boy in the schoolyard. He was wearing a pair of two-buckle plow shoes. Peter could hardly believe it. He looked down at his own satin-calf lace shoes with the nice square toes and then shook his head.

The new boy stood over against the fence with his cap pulled down and a scowl in his dark eyes. He appeared to be about Peter's height, and Peter was nearly as tall as some of the seventh graders. But this boy was more solid, more muscular. Peter imagined this newcomer might be a force to be reckoned with simply because of his size.

As soon as Avery caught sight of the boy, he hollered out, "Hey fellows. Looky there. It's the hayseed who tried to touch my bicycle." More quietly he said, "I hope to heaven he's not in fifth grade."

The boy continued to scowl but said nothing. Peter wished Avery would keep quiet. They went up the wide outside stairs of the school building, through the double doors, and down the hall to put their lunches and books in the fifth-grade classroom.

Later, when class took up, the boy was indeed in fifth grade. Miss Minor, their teacher, was a thin willowy thing with a tiny waspish waist, which appeared even tinier because of her fitted bustle and trim shirtwaist. She introduced the new boy as Harry Dawes, then said to the class, "I know that each of you will go out of your way to make him welcome at Fair Oaks." She gave everyone her nicest smile as she spoke.

Avery snickered out loud. Miss Minor lifted her glasses to her nose from the gold chain about her neck and looked around the room, but she seemed unsure as to where the sound had come from.

"Harry has moved here," she went on, "from Bemidji, where his father sold farm implements. Now Mr. Dawes is the new proprietor of a book bindery downtown. I'm sure we can learn a lot about farming from our new student."

"Yeah," whispered Avery, "like how to get the hayseed out of your hair." The students within hearing all giggled.

"Children, please," Miss Minor said sternly.

From farm implements to a book bindery. Peter turned that around in his mind for a moment but could see no earthly connection. What a strange transition. And why to a neighborhood like Fair Oaks? Odd. Almost like a mystery. A mystery that Peter would love to unravel.

At recess, Avery made sure none of the other boys invited Harry into their game of Pom Pom Pullaway. Heber and Avery were captains and chose up sides. But Harry was off by the fence. He pulled a jackknife from his pocket and proceeded to cut a small branch off the beech tree and sat down on the ground and whittled.

After the teams were chosen, Avery said, "Peter, you

come and count out to see who'll be it."

Peter stepped forward, pointing to first Avery then Heber as he chanted:

"William, William Trembletoe
　Catches hens,
Puts them in pens,
　Wire, briar, limberlock,
Twelve geese in a flock
　Some flew east, some flew west
Some flew over the cuckoo's nest."

Heber was it. He stood in the center of the field as the boys from one side attempted to escape to the other side. Heber yelled out, "Pom pom pullaway. If you don't come, I'll pull you away."

At that call, the boys charged across, and Heber was able to tag three. Peter was one of the first to be tagged because he kept watching the boy in overalls as he whittled with his jackknife. What a strange boy he was. Peter had always wanted a jackknife. He'd seen some of the eighth-grade boys playing mumblety-peg with their knives. Some were very adept at flipping the knives and having them come down right square into a target drawn in the soft dirt.

That evening Peter asked Carol if Harry's sister had been in her class that day. The two of them were sitting on the back steps just before bedtime. Allyson was playing in the hammock that Father had brought out of the toolshed. It was a sure sign of spring when the hammock was once again strung between the two maple trees.

Carol shook her head. "Mattie wasn't there. So Odele and I stopped by her house after school, but her mama said she wasn't feeling well."

"What did she mean by not feeling well?"

"It was sort of odd." Carol screwed up her face as she toyed with one of her long black pigtails.

"Odd, how?"

"Her mama said she'd fallen off the back steps and hurt herself. So I said, 'If she doesn't have anything catching, may we come and see her?' But Mrs. Dawes just shook her head and said, 'I'd rather you not bother her.' "

"Then what?"

"She closed the door."

"Just like that?"

"Just like that. We were going to ask if we could see her tomorrow, but we never got a chance."

The Dawes family was indeed a strange family. Peter wondered again why they chose to move into Fair Oaks.

"Then," Carol added, "as we were leaving, we heard tapping on the upstairs window. There was Mattie looking out the window at us. She had a sad look on her face."

Each day, the girls stopped to see if they could see Mattie. Each day Mrs. Dawes said no. And at school every recess the boys played together without including the new boy. Harry, seemingly unconcerned, sat by himself and whittled. At noon every day, he left the school grounds. Peter assumed he walked home for lunch. Most of the students at Fair Oaks were within walking distance of home, but they all preferred to carry their lunches. A few times during that first week, Avery make offhand remarks to Harry, but the boy ignored them. Harry never smiled.

For the most part, Peter put the whole thing out of his mind. He was looking forward to Saturday morning and his meeting with Grandpa Enoch. Warring emotions swirled inside of him. One moment he was excited, the next moment, he thought it impossible that his old-fashioned Grandpa would ever agree to Peter's having a bicycle.

On Friday after school, the three club members were in the clubhouse talking about what fun they would have on Saturday. As yet, Peter had told neither of them about his appointment with Grandpa. Now that the day had finally arrived, he merely told them he had to meet with his grandpa and left it at that. Neither of his friends asked any questions. They were distracted because Heber was trying to get Avery to agree to let him learn to ride the bicycle. Avery was still noncommittal.

On Saturday morning, Peter was dressed in his nicest double-breasted reefer coat and matching knee pants and his new midshipman's cap with the gold band and gold cord above the shiny bill. Mama had found it on sale at Donaldson's Department Store the week before, and it fit perfectly.

"Mind your manners," Mama told him as she straightened his blouse collar. "I know Grandpa can be gruff at times, but it's just his age. He wasn't always that way."

"I know, Mama." Peter kissed her cheek. "I'd better get going if I'm to catch the trolley and get there on time."

She put her hands on his shoulders and looked at him with her gentle loving eyes. "I can hardly believe you're getting almost as tall as your mama."

Peter chuckled. "That's not very tall, Mama."

Mama laughed along with him as she gave him a giant hug. "Off with you now," she said.

The cold weather of a week ago had been replaced by spring sunshine. Pale tints of green were showing in the towering shade trees along Vine Place as Peter made his way to the trolley stop. He waited for only ten minutes or so before the clanging sounded down the street. Presently the trolley car stopped in front of him. He hopped on, gave his nickel to the conductor, and took a seat by the big open windows.

Rather than get off in front of Grandpa's bank, Peter decided to get off two blocks down Hennepin Street so he could once more see the bicycle in the window of the bicycle shop. It was still there, lovely and shiny as before. He stood for a moment transfixed, staring at it.

"What I wouldn't give. . . ," he whispered to himself. "What fun it would be to whiz around all over Fair Oaks on my very own bicycle. Such freedom!"

He shoved his hands in the pockets of his knee pants and turned to walk up the street to the bank. He opened the heavy door with ornate brass trim and entered the brass and marble foyer. The clock on the wall said nine o'clock. Right on time. That would impress Grandpa.

Peter pulled off his midshipman's cap as he made his way past the grillwork cages of the bank cashiers back to Grandpa's office. Grandpa's secretary, a young man named Josh, greeted Peter with a smile and announced his arrival to his employer.

Presently, Peter was seated in an oversized upholstered chair next to Grandpa's large desk. The giant rolltop desk was awash with papers, books, and ledgers. The dozens of little drawers and cubbyholes were each filled, and some were spilling over. Grandpa's large wooden desk chair creaked as he turned about to face his grandson.

"Peter, my boy, welcome." He pulled out his gold watch from the blue satin vest pocket and snapped open the cover. "Mm, right on time. Punctuality is important." The watch snapped shut again.

Peter smiled. So far, so good.

"Now then," he said, leaning back a bit in the swivel chair. "This is an important year for you, young man. This year of 1896 is your twelfth year. This was the year in the life of the boy Jesus when he first began to show who He was by discoursing with the learned men of the temple. Twelve," he repeated as though it were very important. "The boy was only twelve."

This wasn't the first time Peter had heard these words. Grandpa Enoch had said almost the same thing on New Year's Day last January. Peter didn't figure his twelfth year began until the day of his birthday in September, but Grandpa saw it differently. And truthfully, Peter thought part of all this fuss was simply because he was Grandpa Enoch's oldest grandson.

As Grandpa continued to talk, Peter nodded, smiled, and said "Yes, sir" at appropriate pauses in the conversation.

Finally Grandpa came to the point about the bicycle. "Your father tells me you've seen a bicycle that you want and it costs almost thirty dollars."

"Yes, sir. Twenty-nine dollars," Peter told him.

Grandpa made a tent with his fingers, his elbows propped on the large arms of his chair. "It's good to have a goal to strive for, I believe. That's what stretches a man. Frankly, Peter, I don't think much of these newfangled two-wheeled vehicles. Too dangerous. Boys your age can get into plenty of mischief without a contraption like that to take them farther and farther away from home. But then, who knows what all's coming in this world?" He pointed to the telephone that hung over his desk on a metal rod with the earpiece hanging on the side. "Who'd have thought I'd have a contraption like that thing there hanging on my desk? Just think what we could have done in the war if we'd had telephones. So much better than the telegraph."

"Yes, sir," Peter replied. It *was* an interesting thought.

"So now, you have a goal. But if the thing you want simply falls into your lap, that's not a true goal. It's not a goal unless you strive for it. What's the use of racing down the football field to make a touchdown if you're the only man on the field? What kind of game would that be if there were no resistance?"

Peter thought about that for a moment, but he was uncertain what Grandpa was driving at.

"I'm going to help you get your bicycle, Peter. But my condition is that you earn half the money—earn it on your own—before your twelfth birthday in September."

"Half, sir?"

"Half. You must come up with fifteen dollars."

Peter almost blurted out "Gee whitakers!" but caught himself just in time. Mama would have skinned him alive if he used such language, especially right in front of Grandpa. Fifteen whole dollars. How in the world would he ever earn fifteen dollars in one summer? It seemed utterly impossible. Then he remembered what he'd whispered to himself just a few minutes earlier in front of Holmgren's window: *What I wouldn't give. . .*

What *would* he give to get that bicycle? At least Grandpa didn't say no. Instead, the old man was giving him a chance.

"Well," Grandpa said, "what's your answer? Do we have a deal?"

Though it seemed utterly impossible, Peter heard himself saying, "Yes, sir, we have a deal."

Grandpa reached out his wrinkled hand. "Then let's shake on it—man to man."

Peter stood up and grasped Grandpa's hand, which was still strong and firm in spite of his years. "Thank you, Grandpa Enoch."

"I'll expect you in my office promptly at nine o'clock on the morning of your twelfth birthday. Present to me the fifteen dollars, and we'll go purchase your bicycle."

"I'll do my best."

"That's all I ask." Grandpa turned back to the stacks of papers on his desk, and Peter knew it was time to leave.

CHAPTER 6
The Stevens House

In Peter's pocket were two nickels. One was for the trolley ride home and one Father had given him the night before to buy candy at the store. As Peter walked out of the bank into the brightness of the morning, he quickly decided that he wanted no candy and that he could very well walk home. The ten cents he saved would be the first part of his fifteen dollars. That only left fourteen dollars and ninety cents to go. He groaned at the thought. What an enormous sum of money!

Never had Peter considered having to earn his own

money. Father didn't have much, but he always gave Peter a nickel to spend every now and then. How would he ever explain this to Avery? And how would he have time to enjoy the club and the clubhouse if he had to spend his time earning money?

As he walked home from downtown, he came up with an idea. Perhaps Mama would pay him to watch Mark. When he arrived home, Mama was in the back parlor writing letters at her desk. Carol was practicing the piano, playing scales over and over.

Peter burst into the room. "Mama, I'd like to earn some money. How much would you pay me to take care of Mark for the whole afternoon?"

"Peter," she said, "you startled me. Isn't that a rather ungentlemanly way to enter the room?"

Peter ignored the reprimand. His mind was on other things. "What would it be worth to you? To have me watch Mark for you? Where is he?"

Just then Carol stopped playing and whirled around on the piano stool, making her long braids fly. "What do you mean how much is it worth to watch Mark? What are you talking about?"

"I happen to be addressing Mama," Peter said.

"Peter," Mama chided, "that's no way to talk to your sister."

By now Carol had left the piano and was standing by his side. "Mark's taking a nap. Allyson and I played with him all morning and then Stella fed him a snack and put him to bed. Why are you all of a sudden interested in the baby?"

Peter was beginning to feel a little uncomfortable. "I'm looking for ways to earn money," he said lamely.

"Mama," Carol said with a slight whine in her voice. "That wouldn't be fair. I take care of Mark every day, and no one pays me."

"Now calm down, Carol," Mama said.

Peter shifted his weight from one foot to the other. Caring for Mark didn't seem like such a good idea anymore. He'd have to look somewhere else. But where?

"Never mind," he said, heading back toward the door. "I'm going to find Avery and Heber. See you after awhile."

"Just a minute, young man," Mama said. "You'll have to change clothes first. And aren't you going to tell us how the meeting with Grandpa went?"

"I'll tell you later. I'm in a hurry."

He hurriedly changed into play clothes and hung his nice suit back in the wardrobe. From his bureau drawer he pulled out a small metal box that his set of marbles had come in. In it he dropped the two nickels. This is where he would keep the money he earned. That is, *if* he ever earned any.

On his way out, Mama called to say, "Your father might pay you to clean out the toolshed."

"Thank you, Mama."

Peter ran through the kitchen to grab an apple, then bounded out the back door and down the street toward Shady Lane. When he arrived, Heber was attempting to ride Avery's bicycle. Peter could hardly bear to watch. Avery would push him a ways along the sidewalk, then Heber would wobble and crash to the ground. Avery let out a loud groan.

"You need to pedal harder," Avery told him. "You act like you're afraid of it. All you have to do is just take off." Avery took the bicycle from Heber and examined it closely

51

for scratches. "That's enough for today."

He turned and saw Peter approaching. "Hey, Peter's here," he said. "Now we can have a club meeting." He leaned the bicycle against the tree and never mentioned giving Peter a chance to try to ride. Peter's pride wouldn't allow him to ask. Someday he wouldn't have to ask because he'd have his very own bicycle. It made him even more determined to look for ways to earn fifteen dollars.

"How was the meeting with your grandpa?" Heber wanted to know.

"So–so. You know how grown-ups are." Peter still wasn't sure how his friend would react to this new turn of events. "What have you two been doing?"

"Waiting for you mostly," Heber said. "Avery says he has some nifty news to share."

"Yeah," Avery said. "Wait'll you hear." He led the way inside the clubhouse, and the other two followed.

As they settled down on the carpeting, Avery brought out a copy of the Minneapolis *Journal*. "Listen to this," he said. "A reporter from the *Journal* finally found the old Stevens house."

This was the news? Peter tried not to appear disappointed. "How could anyone lose a house?" he asked as politely as he could. "And why would they want to find it?"

Avery gave him a sour look. "Don't you know how important the Stevens house is? Miss Minor told us about it in history class one day when we were studying Minnesota."

No subject at school was more boring to Peter than history. "I must have been taking a nap," he said.

"You tell him, Heber," Avery said. "You're good with facts."

"Miss Minor said the house was the very first one built on the west side of the Mississippi River almost fifty years ago. She called the house the 'birthplace of Minneapolis.' It's the place where John Stevens laid out the first streets for the city and gave our city its name."

"And named Hennepin County, too, don't forget," Avery added.

"Yeah," Heber said, "and right in the parlor of that house Indian chiefs came and met with the officers from Fort Snelling. Real live Indians." Heber put great emphasis on the "real live" part. Heber was interested in anything that had to do with Indians. When they went to Bear Claw Lake in the summer, Heber was always on the lookout for arrowheads. He now had a good collection.

"My father says Stevens was sort of like a philanthropist because he sold town lots so cheap. Some lots he even gave away so the city would grow."

"It's a real important house," Heber said, "but because it had been moved a couple times, no one knew where it was located. But a *Journal* reporter found it, and now they want to save it."

Peter still wasn't impressed. "Why is that good news for us?"

"You'll hear all about it at school Monday," Avery said, "but because my father knows the editor of the *Journal,* we know about it before any other kids. This," he said shaking the paper with an air of importance, "is a copy of tomorrow's paper."

"Know about what?" Peter asked, growing impatient.

"We're going to help move the house," Avery said.

"We are?" Peter was incredulous. "Move a whole house?

How? Move it where?"

Heber laughed. "Avery means all the schoolkids in the city, not just us. They're going to move the house to Minnehaha Park, where it'll be saved for years to come. And we're going to get the day off school and get free trolley passes and everything."

"With a great big picnic at Minnehaha Falls Park afterward," Avery added.

Peter thought about that for a moment. "Now that sounds like fun. Free trolley passes?"

"And a picnic," Heber added.

"And a day off school." Avery closed the newspaper, a smile spreading across his face.

"When will all this take place?" Peter remembered the apple in his pocket and brought it out and passed it around for each one to take a bite.

Avery opened the paper again. "Thursday, May 28."

"Just a few days before school lets out," Peter said softly.

"It'll be just like having two last days of school," Heber said. "Two fun days almost right in a row."

Yesterday the thought of school letting out for the summer had thrilled Peter. Now everything had changed. It wasn't going to be the usual carefree summer. Moving a house with hundreds of other schoolchildren sounded like a great adventure. But past that, Peter felt as though his entire summer had been spoiled. Why couldn't Father or Grandpa just give him a bicycle like Avery's parents did for him? It just didn't seem fair.

CHAPTER 7

Peter's First Job

Avery was right. The first thing Monday morning, Miss Minor told the fifth graders about the exciting event of moving the Stevens house from the river all the way to Minnehaha Park, six miles away.

The spirit of historic preservation had gripped the entire community, and it seemed as though everyone wanted in on the act. The Minneapolis *Journal* had purchased the old two-story frame house, and in a ceremony at the park, officials from the *Journal* would present the house key to the mayor of the city.

"The house will be mounted on a flatbed," Miss Minor said, reading from a paper in her hand, "and the students will pull the house in seven relays." She looked up from the paper. "We'll know more about our time slot in the relay in a couple weeks." Reading once again, she added, "Teams of workhorses will do the bulk of the pulling."

Avery spoke up and said, "Aw, I bet the schoolkids could pull it easy without any old horses."

Those nearest to Harry Dawes heard him whisper, "Noisy braggart sounds like a braying donkey."

Peter heard him, but he didn't look around to see if Avery had heard it, too.

The news of the house-moving holiday wasn't the only thing of interest that day. The other was that Harry Dawes came to school in different clothes. He was now dressed in a blue wool sailor suit with braid trim and matching knee pants and long stockings. The plow boots were replaced with plain brown oxfords.

Peter took one look at him and decided he looked better in overalls. Because of his size, Harry really looked too old to be wearing knee pants. He appeared uncomfortable in the new clothes and continued to scowl at everyone who looked at him.

Harry's sister was now attending school as well. Peter saw her at recess playing with Odele and Carol. It must have been quite a tumble she took off the back porch. Mattie was a thin little thing with straw-colored braids and a shy smile. Her eye was still a little swollen, and there was an ugly bruise on the side of her face.

As Peter, Avery, and Heber were going across the playground to where they would play Pom Pom Pullaway, they walked by Harry.

As they did, Avery said in a loud voice, "Well, well. Looks like the hayseed found a decent suit of clothes. Do you suppose he found them in a hayloft?"

Heber laughed at the remark.

"At least I'm not a snobbish pig," Harry answered just as loudly.

The voice surprised Peter. It was the first time Harry had spoken up for himself. Peter turned to look at him as he leaned against the fence, knife in hand, slowly whittling. Though the voice sounded full of bitterness, he didn't appear rankled.

But Avery was another story. He turned around and faced Harry. "Who do you think you're calling names?"

Peter took hold of his arm. "Let him be, Avery."

Avery yanked his arm away and took another step. Harry kept whittling, the blade of the knife glinting in the sunshine. "I'd be obliged to take you on, soon's you grow up," Harry said. Acid dripped from every word.

Avery took one more step. Heber and Peter both grabbed him. "Avery," Heber said, his voice shaking, "it's not worth it. You wanna get in trouble this close to the end of the school year? It'd give you bad marks for the whole year."

"The fellas are waiting for us," Peter said, waving toward the area where they played.

Reluctantly Avery turned and went with them. "I don't like that guy," he said through gritted teeth. "He doesn't belong here."

"That's not for you to decide," Peter said firmly. Peter didn't usually disagree with Avery—he'd never really needed to. But after he'd taken his stand, he was glad he had.

That evening the three boys had a good time playing in the clubhouse. The longer it remained light, the longer they were allowed to play in the vacant lot. They had finished a dime novel about swashbuckling pirates, so they decided to play pirates, using the clubhouse as their imaginary ship and grabbing long sticks for their swords.

At twilight Peter walked home, feeling guilty that he was playing rather than looking for work to earn his fifteen dollars. After parting with Heber at the Meeks's house, he happened to notice their neighbor, Widow Daulton, out digging in her spring garden. The sight made him stop in his tracks. Perhaps the widow would pay him to help with her garden.

He lifted the latch on her front gate and went around to the back where she was working. The air was filled with the sweet aroma of freshly turned earth. "Good evening, Widow Daulton," Peter said, lifting his cap politely.

"Oh, Peter. I swan, you gave me a start there. Now what causes you to stop and talk to an old lady? I see you running up and down this sidewalk enough to wear ruts in it." She chuckled at her own joke.

"Well, ma'am, I have a project for which I'm earning money. I was wondering if you would hire me to help you with your garden."

She put a hand to the small of her back. "My son keeps after me to hire a gardener, but for the most part, I like to do the work myself. But this digging is getting to be too much." She adjusted her straw hat, which was decked out in bright flowers. "Could you get this all spaded up before next week?" She waved a wrinkled hand to take in the garden area.

"I sure could," Peter said excitedly. His first paying job. He could hardly believe it. "I'll begin tomorrow right after I get home from school."

"Excellent," replied the widow. "I guess I'd better call it a day. This back of mine is needing a dose of liniment."

By the time Peter was finished with Widow Daulton's garden, his back needed liniment as well. His back ached, his wrists hurt, and his hands were bright red from broken blisters. He could hardly believe that the widow had been doing this work all by herself.

It took three evenings of steady work to get it completed. The widow was a fussy employer. She wanted the ground dug deeply, and all the clods had to be broken up.

Avery and Heber now knew his secret. It was inevitable—Peter knew he couldn't hide it forever. After all, he would be working all summer. At first, Peter gave a lame excuse for why he couldn't join them at the clubhouse, but then Heber saw him in Widow Daulton's yard. Heber ran to get Avery, and when they both approached Peter, he told all. Both his pals were sympathetic.

"Don't let my father hear about this," Heber said. "It'd be just like him to make me do the same thing. And I haven't even asked for a bicycle."

"My father says I'll be working at the mill someday," Avery added, "but not till after I graduate from college. That's a long time from now."

They didn't stick around long, and Peter went back to work.

Mama showed Peter how to soak his hands in Epsom salts to relieve the burning from the broken blisters. "You need a pair of work gloves," she told him after the first night. Together they found a pair of Father's gloves in the toolshed. That helped a little.

When the work was finally completed, Peter went to Widow Daulton to ask for his payment. That was when he realized his first mistake in business—he'd not decided on a price at the outset. The widow invited him into her dim, musty-smelling front parlor, which was crowded with heavy dark furniture, knickknacks, and an amazing array of indoor plants.

She had him wait a moment as she fetched her small leather coin bag. Adjusting her small glasses, she fished around in the bag and finally brought out the coins she was looking for. Into Peter's upturned palm, she dropped two nickels. She gave him a sweet smile and patted his shoulder. "Good job, Peter, my boy. You did a very good job. I may need you to weed my flowers later."

Two nickels. He could hardly believe it. All that work. All that time. "Thank you, Widow Daulton," he said.

In his upstairs bedroom, he took out the tin box and dropped the coins in with the other two nickels. He stared at the four nickels, which looked very small in the large tin. Discouragement hit him all the way down to his toes.

CHAPTER 8
Uncle Abe's Toy

Uncle Abe had a new toy. Mama was right when she said that Uncle Abe had never grown up. Sometimes he and Aunt Elise liked to "borrow" Peter and Carol and Allyson just so Uncle Abe could have fun with his new toys.

"He calls it a magic lantern," Mama explained. She'd just hung up the receiver of the big wooden telephone that hung on the kitchen wall. They were finishing up supper on Friday evening. "He called to invite you children to come and watch a magic lantern show."

Peter adored Uncle Abe's gadgets. "When?" he asked. "Now?"

"As soon as you can get your hats and coats on and get over there," Mama answered.

Allyson was jumping up and down and whirling in circles, her pinafore flowing out as she spun. Mama made her return to her seat and clean up her plate before she could go.

"I can't eat when I'm excited," Allyson retorted. But she finished her supper—and quickly, too.

Peter was excited as well. After his first week of discouraging employment, he needed a little fun. When Mama was satisfied that each child looked trim and neat, the three walked to Uncle Abe's house.

Aunt Elise met them at the door with her usual cheery smile. After giving each one a hug, she ushered them into the back parlor. "Your uncle is still experimenting with his magic lantern," she told them. "So you are his guinea pigs."

"I don't want to be a pig," Allyson protested. "Pigs stink." She took off her little sailor hat with the elastic band that fit under her chin. She handed it to Aunt Elise along with her coat.

"No, no, Allyson," Carol corrected her. "Guinea pigs are furry little animals that are used in experiments. She means that Uncle Abe wants to test the magic lantern on us."

"Oh." Allyson fairly bounced through Aunt Elise's big house.

Peter had a fair idea what it was, for he'd read of magic lanterns in the advertisements in his *Youth Companion* magazine.

"Ho there, kiddos," came Uncle Abe's booming welcome as they entered the room. On a small table he'd set up his apparatus, and on one wall hung a white bedsheet where he was going to project his show. The lantern looked like a large box camera with a telescope sticking out the front and a chimney on top.

"Come see," he said, waving them over. The three of them clustered around the table, staring in amazement.

Allyson wrinkled her nose. "It smells like a kerosene lamp."

"Exactly," Uncle Abe answered. He lit the lamp inside. "This is designed to condense the light of the lamp through this opening." He pointed to the telescoping part on the front.

"Then what does it do?" Carol asked.

Uncle Abe held up a small glass plate. "See the picture on this piece of glass?"

Allyson took it from his hand. "It's almost too tiny to see."

Peter could see that the etchings on the glass were colored. It appeared to be a man on a horse.

"Now watch the sheet," Uncle Abe told them. He slipped the glass slide into the magic lantern, and all of a sudden, the colored picture of the man on a horse was on the sheet as big as life. The round picture was nearly four feet across. Allyson and Carol gasped. Peter couldn't say a word. It was amazing. No wonder it was called magic.

"Look at this," said Aunt Elise. She held up a small pasteboard box that was full of slides all neatly fitted into pasteboard slots.

"Gee whitakers!" Peter said, then slapped his hand over his mouth. "Excuse me," he said. Carol frowned, but Uncle Abe laughed.

"Now which would you like to see first?" he asked. "I have landscapes of Venice, Germany, Russia, and Jerusalem."

"Jerusalem," Allyson called out, bouncing on her toes. "That's where Jesus was."

Aunt Elise let them sit on the floor in front of the sheet, and they not only saw scenes from Jerusalem, but all the other cities as well. Then there were action slides. When Uncle Abe moved the slide quickly from one position to the next, it looked as though a bushwhacker were jumping from behind a rock to attack a stagecoach. Allyson squealed with excitement every time it moved.

Running to Uncle Abe's side, she asked, "When my birthday comes in the summer, may I have a magic lantern show for my party?"

"You certainly may, my little pet," Uncle Abe told her. He swept her up in his arms and gave her a big hug. "You certainly may."

At that moment, Carleen, their cook, came in to let them know that lemonade and cookies were ready. Uncle Abe turned the wick down on the magic lantern, making the light go out. Aunt Elise thanked Carleen, saying they were all ready for refreshments after such an exciting evening.

The ruddy-cheeked Carleen O'Callaghan with curly, copper-colored hair was new to the Stevenson household, and she spoke with a soft Galway brogue.

"She'd not been in the country long when her husband died," Aunt Elise told them after Carleen left the room. "What a tragedy since she has a little girl to care for."

"I'm glad we found her," Uncle Abe said. "She seems to fit perfectly here. She's comfortable living above the carriage house. And wait'll you see her little girl, Maureen—

cute as a bug's ear."

Later as they sat around the parlor enjoying the tasty cookies, Carol noticed a photograph on Aunt Elise's sideboard. Walking over to get a closer look, she asked, "Isn't this a new photograph? This looks like Miss Frances Willard."

"It is at that, Carol."

"And you're in the photograph beside her. When were you with her?" Carol wanted to know.

The family knew Aunt Elise was an avid follower of this world-famous woman, but it wasn't talked about around the other adults. Miss Willard, as national president of the WCTU, was more famous than President Cleveland's wife.

"Bring it here," Aunt Elise said, "and I'll tell you more."

Carol brought the photograph over to where Aunt Elise was sitting on the damask-covered davenport. Carol sat on one side and Peter on the other, with Allyson in Aunt Elise's lap.

"This is only one of several photographs I have of Miss Willard," Aunt Elise said, "but of course I don't put them all out."

"Why?" Allyson wanted to know. "Isn't she a nice lady?"

"She's a very nice lady, Allyson. But she has many ideas that some people don't always agree with."

"Like what?" Carol asked.

"Like women wearing bicycle suits and riding bicycles," Aunt Elise said with a smile.

Carol gave the photograph a closer look. "Does she ride a bicycle? She looks so old."

"Not only does she ride a bicycle," Aunt Elise said, "but she also wrote a book about the benefits of bicycle-riding as exercise."

Uncle Abe was putting the slides back in their box. "But bicycle riding is not all Miss Willard believes in."

"Oh no," Aunt Elise said. "She believes that women should be allowed to vote and that the selling of liquor should be against the law."

Peter thought of the many saloons in the city. He didn't wonder that many men didn't care to hear about Miss Willard.

"Tell us about meeting her," Carol said.

"I've met with her on several occasions. I've been to the WCTU headquarters in Chicago, and last year I was invited to her home in Evanston, Illinois. She calls the place Rest Cottage, but it doesn't seem much rest goes on there. She has several secretaries and works tirelessly for all her causes."

Carol flipped a dark braid back over her shoulder. "What's she like, Aunt Elise? I mean, what's she really like?"

"Kind and most gracious," Aunt Elise told her.

"Is Miss Willard the reason why you work at the mission?" Peter asked.

Aunt Elise nodded. "In a way it is, Peter. Some of Miss Willard's first work was in The Loop in Chicago, where she and other women operated a mission for the down-and-out drunkards in the area. They ministered with hot meals, clean clothing, and the gospel of Jesus Christ. That's where I learned how to organize the work and how to carry it out."

Carol gave a little shiver. "Aren't you scared to be down on skid row?"

"God protects me," Aunt Elise assured her, "just as he would if I were a missionary in a foreign land."

"And don't forget old Uncle Abe prays for her," Uncle Abe put in.

"I'm glad no old drunks live in our nice neighborhood," Allyson said.

"But that's just it," Aunt Elise said. "Drunkards aren't only in the poorer section of town. There are those who are chained to the power of demon rum in nicer neighborhoods, too, but no one can tell at first glance. It's a well-hidden secret."

"What happens?" Carol wanted to know.

"Most often the man in the family becomes violent and hurts the children and the mother. A drunk man doesn't know what he's doing. He says and does things that he doesn't remember after the alcohol loses its effect."

Uncle Abe came over, scooted up the tufted hassock, and sat down opposite them. "Oddly enough, Miss Willard has two nephews who have problems with alcohol, as did her brother before he died."

Carol shook her head. "How perfectly dreadful."

"That's part of the reason why Miss Willard has worked so hard to advance the cause of the WCTU," Aunt Elise said. "Now there are hundreds of thousands of members all across the country. And I'm proud to be one of them."

"I'm going to join the WCTU when I grow up," Carol announced.

Peter tried to imagine Father drinking too much and becoming angry at them, but it was impossible to fathom such a thing. As far as Peter knew, Father had never touched alcohol.

Carol changed the subject then and began to tell Aunt Elise and Uncle Abe all about the upcoming adventure of moving the Stevens house. Peter knew that Uncle Abe had probably read all about it in the *Journal,* but that didn't stop the man from listening politely to every detail as though he'd never heard. Uncle Abe was a very special person.

Soon the wonderful evening drew to a close, and it was time to go home. They thanked Uncle Abe over and over for the magic lantern show.

"And for telling us all about Miss Frances Willard," Carol added, giving her aunt a hug.

They stepped outside into a perfect moonlit spring evening, with just a touch of breeze. As Peter walked down the sidewalk behind his sisters, he thought about the magic lantern. That apparatus probably cost as much as two or three bicycles. How he wished he had as much money to spend as Uncle Abe had.

At school the next week, excitement about the moving of the Stevens house was mounting. Miss Minor had the schedules that told them what time they were to board the trolleys, meet up with the traveling house, and take their turn pulling the cables.

The boy who sat in front of Peter, Albert Kingsbury, told Miss Minor that the teams of horses being used were to come from his father's livery stable. Peter knew right where that livery was located at the corner of Nicollet and Seventh. He passed it every time he went downtown.

Miss Minor pointed to a large street map of the city, hanging on the wall. She explained that the house would be moved from Sixteenth Avenue South, between Third and Fourth Streets, all the way to Minnehaha Avenue at Fiftieth Street in the park.

"Our group," she said, meaning Fair Oaks Grammar School, "will board the trolley at ten in the morning and meet up with the house at Twenty-Fifth Street." A twitter of voices sounded through the room as they all thought how much fun it would be to help pull the cables and roll that house down the streets of Minneapolis.

Their turn, Miss Minor told them, would coincide with South High School, which was where Martin and Naomi attended. At the end of the journey, when the house arrived at the park, there was to be a citywide picnic with band music and speeches.

Peter glanced over at Harry, who was slouched down in his seat. Peter guessed it didn't sound very exciting to some-one like Harry Dawes. The boy was a terrible grouch.

"Sounds like more fun than the Fourth of July," Heber said later that day as they ran outside for recess.

"Nothing is more fun than the Fourth of July," Avery replied.

"Well, this might be," Heber countered. "We don't know because we've never moved a house before."

"At least we get a day off school," Peter reminded them. He was more than ready for school to be out.

Out on the schoolyard, he noticed Mattie Dawes playing skip rope with a group of the girls. They were singing a chant as Mattie helped turn one end of the rope:

"Lady, lady, turn around
  Lady, lady, touch the ground
Lady, lady, touch your shoe
  Lady, lady, twenty-three skiddoo."

At the word *skiddoo,* the girl who was jumping scooted out and another ran in. Peter watched a moment and wondered why Mattie seemed to fit in while her grouchy brother didn't. That evening he decided to talk with Carol about the family.

"Do you girls ever play at the Dawes house?" he asked.

Carol shook her head. "Mattie's never invited us there. Somehow Odele and I get the feeling she doesn't want us to go inside her house."

Stella nearly had supper ready, and the aromas of her shepherd's pie floated through the house. Carol had just finished her piano practice when Peter cornered her. He leaned against the piano and watched as she folded up her music and put it away in the music cabinet.

"Why do you think that is?"

She shrugged as she closed the doors on the cabinet. "All I know is when they moved in there wasn't much furniture. It's almost as though she's ashamed."

"Why would a man who sold farm implements suddenly switch over to a book bindery?" he wondered aloud.

"That's easy. They inherited the business from their mother's uncle who recently died."

Peter leaned forward at this tidbit of information. "You don't say. Tell me more."

"That's all I know. Mattie said her mama didn't want to move from Bemidji. She hated to leave all her friends behind, but her father insisted."

"Did they receive money in the inheritance as well?"

"She didn't say. It isn't nice to ask such things, you know."

"Is Mattie as sour as her brother? She seems to get along with her classmates better than Harry does."

Just then, Stella called them to supper.

Carol stood and smoothed the ruffles of her pink dress

and adjusted the puffy sleeves. Going out of the room ahead of Peter, she quipped, "Perhaps it's because we've treated Mattie nicer than you boys ever treated Harry."

Peter thought about that a moment. He realized she could be right.

CHAPTER 9

The House Moving

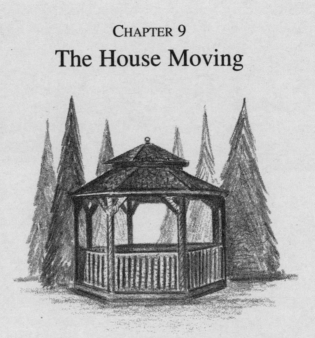

It rained the few days preceding house-moving day, but May 28 dawned with a cloudless sky. Father planned to leave the bank early and return home and fetch Mama and Mark and come to the park and join in the festivities. The whole town had proclaimed it a holiday. Hundreds of people were planning to line the streets along the way to watch the procession.

In Miss Minor's classroom, the stern teacher was having

difficulty keeping order. At last she agreed to let the students talk if they did so in whispers. By midmorning they were lined up on the sidewalks in front of the school, waiting as several trolley cars came to a stop. Then all the students clambered aboard.

There were seven relay stops along the way, and theirs was the second stop. Heber, Avery, and Peter crowded into one seat with Peter scrunched against the window. As they approached Twenty-fifth Street, Peter craned his neck to see the large house moving slowly along the street surrounded by students both elementary age and high school. Two teams of big workhorses grandly pulled at a steady pace. In front of the horses were clusters of students pulling on the cables.

Peter pointed out the window. "Is that what everybody's making such a fuss about? It looks terrible."

And indeed it did. The two-story frame house was dilapidated. Its windows were broken out, and the doors hung off their hinges. Peter was amazed that they would go to so much trouble—it was just an old house.

As the trolley stopped, the Fair Oaks students piled off and ran toward the flatbed wagon. At the same time, more trolley cars arrived with students from South High School. According to plan, the first set of students boarded the empty trolley cars and were taken on to Minnehaha Park.

Several of the high school boys began chanting their school rally calls. Not satisfied with simply pulling the cables, they jumped up on the wagons and went into the house to hang their colors from the upstairs windows.

"Look," Avery said to Heber. "There's your brother."

Sure enough, Martin was one of the culprits waving out

73

the windows and shouting the rally calls. Peter laughed at
the sight. He grabbed hold of a cable, which turned out to be
a fire hose, and began pulling along with the rest. Avery was
in front of him and Heber behind him. Since most of the
Fair Oaks students would eventually attend South High,
they gladly joined in the chants with the high school kids.

Suddenly there was Harry Dawes. He grabbed hold of
the fire hose just ahead of Avery. Peter was sure he had
chosen that position on purpose.

"Hey, there," Avery called out sharply. "You're in my
way."

"He's not in your way," Peter said in a low voice. "Just
leave him alone."

"No, I won't. He's pushing in where he doesn't belong."
Peter glanced back at Heber. Heber shrugged.

At first, Harry ignored Avery. But Avery wasn't satisfied. He let go of the cable and gave Harry a shove.

The boy stumbled a few steps, then whirled around with
fire in his eyes. "You've been asking for this for a long
time," he said. Fast as lightning, he faked a punch with his
right fist. The moment Avery dodged, Harry slammed him
with his left. Avery Norton went flying onto the street. Avery
had been practicing boxing at the country club. Evidently
he'd not practiced enough.

Several policemen were walking along with the
entourage, and one came up at that moment. "What's going
on here?" he demanded.

"He hit me!" Avery called out, pointing to Harry.

The kindly policeman walked over to Harry and put his
arm about his shoulder. "Now young man, it's not good to
be fighting on such a fine holiday as this. Come now, let's

find a different place for you where you'll not be getting into trouble."

Peter wondered if the policeman had seen more than he let on, because he didn't pay attention to Avery at all. Peter and Heber had run to help Avery to his feet, but he waved them away.

"Aw go on," he growled. "I can get up by myself. It wasn't much of a punch anyway." But he was rubbing his jaw and rubbing it hard.

Peter said nothing, but his mind was swirling. As he went back to the cables to continue pulling the house down the street, he thought of how he and Avery had been friends since before they were in first grade. By rights, he should be siding with his friend, but in this situation he knew Avery was wrong. Dead wrong.

In no time at all, they arrived at the next relay point. Students from Central High School arrived on the trolleys, along with students from other grammar schools. When the Central High boys saw the South High boys up in the house, they began to shout, ordering them to get out and make way.

Perhaps it was how the Central boys made the demands that caused the South High students to stand fast. But no matter—the result was a standoff confrontation between the bitter arch rivals. Peter had let go of the cable and was preparing to board the trolley. Now he saw there were not only boys up in the house, but girls as well. And there was Naomi Norton.

Before anyone could blink, the confrontation turned into a wild melee. Students were pushing and shoving and yelling. "Come on," Peter said to Avery. "Your sister's in there."

He ran toward the wagon and felt himself getting roughly pushed and shoved. The yelling was deafening. Avery yelled at Naomi. "Over here, Naomi." He stretched up his hands. But she was being pummeled by the onslaught of Central boys, most of whom came from the rougher side of town.

Suddenly, Martin came out of the house. He made his way toward Naomi, lifted her up in his arms, and pushed through the crowd to the end of the wagon and got her safely down.

The kindly policeman who'd taken Harry away was trying to bring order, but the boys hooted at him and shoved him back out the door of the house. Within minutes, reinforcements arrived, and at last the noise subsided and peace and order were restored.

When they were finally on the trolley, Peter, Heber, and Avery saw Martin in the very back seat, sitting with his arm around Naomi. Peter guessed Martin wouldn't have to work so hard to get her attention after this.

At the park, a brass band was in the bandstand playing rousing march tunes, and great tubs of lemonade were being served to the hundreds of thirsty students. By late afternoon, a cheer arose from the crowd as the house appeared at the edge of the park. A special speaker's platform had been constructed for the presentation. Peter and his pals sat under a shade tree to listen.

Fred Snyder, a man who'd been born in the famous house, told ever so many details of the historic events that took place there—how territorial court had been conducted in the parlor and how the Minnesota State Fair and the first school district in Minneapolis were formed there.

As the speeches continued, Peter finally understood why

such a house should be preserved. And he was proud to have been a part of that preservation—in spite of all the scuffling that had taken place along the way.

An official from the *Journal* presented the key to the house to Mayor Fred Pratt. Heber laughed. "There's no need for a key with all the doors falling off."

"It's ceremonial," Peter said, poking Heber in the ribs with his elbow. "It's not supposed to really unlock the doors."

"Well, don't get testy with me. I was just making a joke."

After the presentations, the three boys split up to find their families, who had brought loaded picnic baskets.

Mama had told Peter that morning that they would meet him and Carol at the bandstand. Pushing through the press of people, Peter happened to see Albert Kingsbury. Along with his brother, he was leading the big workhorses who'd done most of the house-moving work.

"Hey, Albert," Peter called out.

Albert stopped. "Hello, Peter. Where're you going?"

"To meet up with my family and eat. May I pet your horses?"

"Sure." Albert had a set of harness reins in each hand. "Whoa," he said in a deep voice, and the big horses halted. They were bigger than most dray horses that pulled delivery wagons about the city.

Peter reached up and petted the soft nose. In spite of his great size, the horse had kind eyes. "These are the real heros of the day," Peter remarked.

Albert laughed. "That's what Jerry and I were just saying." The horses stood perfectly still. "Peter," Albert said, "this is my older brother, Jerry. He's a senior at South High."

Peter couldn't shake hands with Jerry since his hands were filled with harnesses. "Are they your horses?"

"Actually we rented these from a wheat farmer from out in the country," Albert explained. "We don't need horses this big in the city."

"I bet it's fun to work with them."

"It is," Albert replied, "if you like horses."

"I'd like to live out West where everyone owns a horse," Peter told him. He thought of the dime novels he'd read. Every character had his own horse.

"So, you like horses, too?"

Peter nodded. "I like most all kinds of animals." He started to go then, but a sudden thought came to his head. "Say, Albert, your father wouldn't need an extra hand at the livery, would he?"

Albert looked at his brother, then back at Peter. "Who's looking?"

"I am."

Albert's eyebrows went up. "You?"

Peter nodded. He knew it was a surprise. Almost all the kids thought Peter's family was rich just because his father worked at the bank. "Actually," he said, "I have a challenge from my grandpa. I need to earn money through the summer. If I earn enough, he'll go half on a bicycle with me for my birthday in September."

"Sounds like you have a nice grandpa," Jerry said.

Peter let that remark pass. "So do you need help?"

"We just lost a boy last week. He started selling newspapers downtown," Jerry said. "Papa hasn't replaced him yet, but I know he needs to."

Suddenly, Peter's heart made a little skip.

"Why don't you come over on Saturday and talk with Papa." Jerry pulled on the harness reins and turned to go. Over his shoulder, he added, "I'll tell him to expect you."

"I'll be there," Peter said, waving as the two brothers walked off. "I'll be there first thing Saturday morning. And thanks."

As Peter turned toward the bandstand to find his family, he was filled with amazement. Not only did he have a possible job, but he was actually excited about it.

CHAPTER 10
Rags

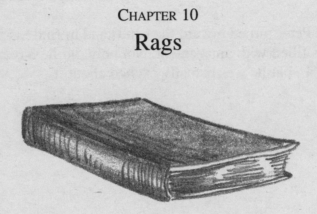

The school commencement exercises had been eclipsed by moving the Stevens house. The evening program in the Fair Oaks school auditorium was nice, but nothing could match that citywide celebration in Minnehaha Park for fun and excitement.

Fair Oaks Grammar School was crowded with parents and families on commencement night. Neither Peter nor his two pals had received any special awards. Nor had they been chosen to give special recitations. So it was rather boring for them—more so since they had to wear their church clothes.

Carol and Odele were to play a piano duet, and they were nervous as bedbugs. Peter just wanted to stay away from them.

In the halls, girls were running around with their leather-bound autograph books, asking all their friends to write little notes and poems in them. The eighth-grade girls especially were beside themselves with excitement. They were decked out in lacy white dresses with silk pastel sashes.

Graduating from grammar school into high school was a big step. Thankfully that was many long years away for Peter. For his part, he was pleased when the whole commencement thing was over and done with. His mind was set on his appointment at Kingsbury Livery on Saturday morning.

The meeting with Mr. Kingsbury went famously. When Peter first saw the tall, broad-shouldered man, he was somewhat intimidated. However, once they began talking, Peter could tell the livery owner was not at all gruff. Peter was hired on the spot. Mr. Kingsbury offered him four hours of work a day, six days a week, at a nickel an hour starting Monday morning.

After thanking Mr. Kingsbury, Peter rushed home and put pencil to paper. He would earn $1.20 a week. For two weeks in August, he would be with his family at the lake cabin, so that left twelve weeks to work before school started. From his figures, it looked as though he would earn $14.40 in that time.

That was close enough. Perhaps he could earn the difference doing odd jobs around the neighborhood. He closed the notebook with a satisfied smile and tucked it in the bureau drawer along with his money tin. The royal blue bicycle was as good as his.

When he told Avery and Heber about his job during Sunday school the next day, they both groaned.

"Now we'll never have any fun this summer," Heber

said. "What about the club?"

"I work from seven in the morning until eleven. I'll have every afternoon free," Peter explained patiently. It was difficult to explain to them how pleased he was about the whole arrangement.

Avery shook his head. "You won't ever get to sleep late."

"I don't mind. I like to get up early anyway."

And he did. On his first day of work, he was out of bed and downstairs for breakfast before Father. Peter was determined to be on time. When Father came downstairs, he asked Peter if they would be riding the trolley together.

"No, sir," Peter said. "I'll walk. I can't afford to spend the nickel for the trolley every day and still make the fifteen dollars."

Father looked pleased and surprised. "You seem very serious about this deal with your grandpa."

"I want that blue bicycle," he said, "in the worst way."

When Peter arrived for work, Albert took one look at him and started laughing. "Are you going to work in those clothes?" he asked. "They'll be in tatters in two days."

Peter had on his cotton play clothes that he usually wore through the summer months. But Albert and Jerry were wearing denim dungarees and chambray work shirts. It never occurred to Peter that he didn't have the right clothes for working in a livery.

"That's all right," Albert said. "You and I are about the same size. I probably have a pair of dungarees that'll fit you." Mr. Kingsbury telephoned his wife, and within the hour Mrs. Kingsbury arrived with work clothes for Peter to change into. It was kind of them, but now Peter wondered if some of his salary would have to go to buy clothes.

As Albert showed him how to muck out the stalls and how to spread clean hay in its place, Peter thought about Harry. He remembered how Avery had made fun of his overalls. When Albert had laughed at Peter's play clothes, in a very small way Peter had known how Harry felt.

Mr. Kingsbury was a strict employer but a fair one. He expected the work to be done right and the horses to be well cared for. He allowed no mistreatment of any animal that he owned. Peter quickly came to respect the man.

After Peter's first day, he talked with Father about the clothes he would need.

"I see no reason why we can't purchase your work clothes," Father said. "While I can't afford a bicycle, I can at least afford to keep you clothed."

Peter continued to wear Albert's clothes that first week, then Peter and Mama went to Donaldson's on Saturday afternoon to shop. Of course Carol and Allyson had to come along. Stella kept Mark at home.

Donaldson's was the largest department store for miles around. The magnificent five-story building was capped with a corner dome with a lookout tower way up on top. All three Morgan children loved a trip to Donaldson's.

The girls got new wash dresses for a summer of outdoor playing. After purchasing Peter's new dungarees, work shirts, and a pair of sturdy oxfords, they had lunch in the restaurant that was located right in the store. The four of them arrived home exhausted but happy from a full day of shopping. Now Peter would not be wearing knee pants each day. It was rather a grown-up feeling to go to work in his dungarees.

By the second week, Peter had learned a great deal and

was carrying his own weight in the livery. He walked home each day with a feeling of satisfaction. At the end of the second week, $2.40 from his wages was added to the twenty cents that sat in the tin box. He kept a running total of his income in a small notebook.

Every afternoon was spent playing with Avery and Heber. The days were full of climbing trees, floating home-made boats on the lake in the park, playing baseball, and reading dime novels in the clubhouse.

Martin and Naomi spent a great deal of time together, so it became great sport for the Shady Vinewood Club members to find the unsuspecting couple—usually in the gazebo in the Norton's backyard—and tease and torment them.

Toward the middle of June, Aunt Elise privately asked Peter if he would like to learn to ride her bicycle. "I know it's a lady's bicycle," she said, "but I believe you could use the area behind our house and no one would see you."

Peter could hardly believe his good fortune. Aunt Elise was so smart. She knew he wouldn't want Avery or Heber to see him on a lady's bicycle. With just a few short lessons and with Uncle Abe holding the bicycle to steady him, he quickly got the hang of it. More than ever, Peter was ready for his own bicycle.

One overcast June day, Peter was walking home from the livery in a gray drizzle. As he passed a row of thick spirea bushes a few blocks from his house, he thought he heard whining. He stopped to listen, but it must have been his imagination. He walked on.

After a moment he heard it again. He began to look in the thick bushes along the sidewalk, lifting the arching branches to peer beneath. Getting down on his hands and knees on the wet ground, he finally saw the source of the noise. A brown and white dog lay under the thick bushes, all curled up in a tight ball. Their eyes met. The dog's soft brown eyes didn't show a bit of fear.

"Hello there, fella. Are you lost?" Peter edged farther under the bushes. He reached out his hand to touch the dog's head. Still there seemed to be no fear. Now Peter could see that the fur was mangy and unkempt. "Poor thing," Peter said softly. "Are you hurt?"

As he attempted to move the dog, the animal whimpered. It seemed that his back leg was hurt. Carefully, slowly, Peter eased the dog closer and closer until he was able to get his arms positioned to lift him. Since Peter was already dirty from working at the livery, he didn't mind that the dog was all muddy, and he carried the poor thing all the way home.

When he reached home, Peter went around to the back door. Because of the rain, Carol and Allyson were on the sunporch playing paper dolls. They dropped everything when they saw what he had in his arms.

"A puppy, a puppy!" Allyson said, jumping up and down.

"It's bigger than a puppy," Peter told her. "Go get Mama and ask her to bring some old towels."

Allyson ran to do as he asked. Soon they had the dog lying in a corner of the sunporch on a pile of old towels. Peter was trying his best to clean off the mud and see how badly the leg was hurt. There was no open wound, and the leg didn't appear to be broken.

"It must just be bruised," Peter said.

"Poor thing," Mama cooed. "I wonder if someone lost him?"

"I'll ask around the neighborhood," Peter said. Then

looking up at Mama, he said, "If no one claims him, may I keep him?"

"Oh yes, Mama," Allyson chimed in. "May we? We've never had a dog before."

Mama pursed her lips and thought. "I'm not sure what your father will say. Let's wait and see."

"He really looks ragtag, doesn't he?" Carol said. "Like he's been on his own for quite some time."

Peter smiled. "Ragtag. I like that, Carol. I think I'll call him Rags."

Peter asked around the neighborhood, but no one had lost a dog. And no one came looking for a dog. Then, best of all, Father gave permission for Peter to keep Rags. With a bath and plenty of good food—mostly scraps from Stella's kitchen—Rags began to fill out. His coat grew glossy and thick. The white became whiter, and the brown spots became the color of chocolate.

He followed Peter everywhere. It was as though he knew Peter had saved his life. He followed Peter to the livery each day and then curled up in the hay in a corner and bothered no one until it was time to go home.

"You'd better get a collar for that dog," Mr. Kingsbury told Peter one day. "If he got lost once, he might get lost again."

Peter hadn't thought of that. So the next afternoon he visited the hardware store and with twenty cents of his hard-earned money purchased a collar and tag. The man at the hardware store engraved the name "Rags" on the metal tag, along with the Morgans' telephone number.

There in the hardware store, Peter knelt down and buckled the woven collar on Rags's neck, then ruffled his soft coat and hugged him close. "There you go, fella. Now everyone will know who you are and where you belong."

As Peter walked home with Rags trotting by his side, he felt as though the dog was now officially his. He tried not to worry too much about the twenty cents he'd spent. Rags was worth that and more.

The neighborhood of Fair Oaks had a number of summer birthdays among the children. It seemed there was a birthday party every other week.

"I wish my birthday were in summer," Carol confided to Peter one day.

It wasn't the first time Peter had heard his sister's lament. She hated having her birthday on Christmas Day. "Just think," Peter tried to reassure her, "the whole world celebrates on your birthday."

She frowned. "That's just it. My birthday is always lost in the shuffle. That's no fun."

Odele Meeks had a big party in her backyard, with balloons and blocks of ice cream shaped like clowns. They melted almost before they were eaten, but it was still fun. She received a pair of roller skates, which Carol kept staring at.

The next week, Odele was skating up and down the sidewalks of Fair Oaks. Being the generous person she was, she would sometimes share one skate with Carol. "We'll skate single-legged," Odele said. The two of them raced as fast as one skate could go, giggling all the way.

Mattie attended Odele's party, but no one had seen much of Harry since school let out. Peter was too embarrassed to ask about him.

The next party was for Allyson. She turned six at the end of June. As promised, Uncle Abe put on a magic lantern show. This one was even better. He and Aunt Elise hung the bedsheet out in the backyard against the door of the carriage house. Chairs and tables had been set up on the back lawn, and large blankets were spread out for the children to sit on. The weather was sticky hot with not a breath of breeze blowing.

Mama had agreed to allow the party to be held at Uncle Abe's house, and almost a dozen children attended. Allyson was bouncing around everywhere. Peter had never seen her so excited. To think this show was all for her. Uncle Abe surprised her with a special slide that cast the words *Happy Birthday* in brilliant red on the bedsheet. All the children gasped just as the Morgan children had done when they first saw the magic lantern work.

This show lasted longer than the first one because now Uncle Abe had more slides. Peter, Avery, and Heber were sitting on a blanket near the row of lilac bushes. Rags was curled up contentedly.

In the middle of the show, Peter got up to get more punch. As he did, he saw movement out of the corner of his eye. Through the lilacs he glimpsed a figure. His first instinct was to yell, but he stopped just in time. It was Harry Dawes. Peter turned away and acted as though he saw nothing. He refilled his cup and returned to the blanket and watched the rest of the show.

Deep inside Peter, something ached for Harry because the boy had to watch the wonderful magic lantern show from behind the lilac bushes. He knew it wasn't right.

Late that evening they walked home. Mark was sleeping

peacefully in his pram, which Mama was pushing, and Allyson slept on Father's shoulder.

"It was a lovely party," Mama said. "Abe is so good to the children."

Father agreed. "He seems to have a knack with them."

"He's been working with the boys at the YMCA downtown." Mama stopped to spread a light blanket over Mark since a breeze had come up. "How many childless men do you know would do such a kind and selfless thing?"

"There could never be an outdoor magic lantern show on Christmas Day," Carol murmured softly.

"Now, Carol," Mama chided. "Let's not go into that again. Every birthday is special, no matter when it comes."

Off in the distance, lightning zigzagged sharply through the clear night sky and thunder rumbled softly. Rags made a whining noise deep in his throat.

"We'd better hurry," Father said. "Looks like a bad storm's building up."

CHAPTER 11

Secret in the Clubhouse

The storm came crashing into the city just after midnight. Thunder exploded. Lightning flashed bright as day. Peter put a pillow over his head to keep out the noise. He heard Allyson calling for Mama. Then he heard Mama going down the hall to Allyson's room.

Suddenly he sat straight up. Rags! Rags was inside the sunporch. Would the dog be scared of the storm?

Leaping from his bed, Peter took the stairs two at a time and landed with a thud in the hallway. He ran through the house, back to the sunporch. "Rags!" he called out.

He switched on the electric light, but nothing happened.

The storm had caused the electricity to go out. Another flash of lightning was enough to show there was no dog on the porch. Peter went to the door. A hole was torn in the screen. The frightened dog must have jumped through.

Opening the screen, Peter stood out on the stoop and called as loudly as he could. Rags did not come. He'd have to go looking, Peter decided. Rags couldn't have gone far.

He ran back upstairs to pull on his dungarees and work shoes. That would be best for a night like this. His rain slicker was in the downstairs hall closet. As he came out of his bedroom, he almost ran into Father. He'd fetched a lantern and was lighting it.

"Where do you think you're going, young man?"

"Rags broke through the screen door. I've got to go find him."

"You can't go out in this storm. It's too dangerous." This from Mama who was now standing by Father's side. Her flowered wrapper was pulled about her, and her long chestnut-colored hair fell over her shoulders.

"I have to go, Mama. Rags is depending on me. Don't you see? I *have* to."

Father put his hand on Mama's arm. "Let him go, Polly. It's important to him. We'll trust the Lord to watch over him."

"Thank you, Father." Peter flew downstairs, grabbed his rain slicker, and was out the back door before they could change their minds.

The rain came slashing down out of the sky, and the ferocious wind whipped it every which way. Peter pulled the slicker tightly about him and pressed against the wind, calling Rags's name over and over. He went up one block and down the other. He looked in every hedge and bush he came to. There was no sign of the chocolate-colored dog.

"Where could he be?" Peter mumbled to himself. Then he said, "Lord, You know Rags. You know what a good dog he is. You brought him to me in the first place. Please keep him safe for me and let me find him."

After praying, Peter tried to think of every place in the neighborhood that the dog knew. Where might he go to get in out of the wet and cold? Suddenly it came to him. He ran all the way down Vine Place to Shady Lane. He ran the length of the vacant lot to the big oak tree. Could it be?

Slowly he opened the door of the clubhouse. The tar paper roof had worked perfectly. Inside was warm and dry. And there curled up on the carpeting was Rags. Peter stood and stared in disbelief. Beside Rags lay Harry Dawes with his arm around the dog.

Harry's eyes grew wide as he stared back. "Rags was running frightened out in the rain," he said softly. "So I brought him in here. I hope it was okay."

"Thank you," Peter croaked.

Harry had no jacket, no rain slicker. He was wet, and his hair was matted worse than Rags's was. "Why not come in and close the door?" Harry suggested, moving to a sitting position.

Peter nodded, ducked his head, and entered. Rags whined and came over, laying his head in Peter's lap. "Hello, fella. You're scared of storms, aren't you?" Peter stroked the wet fur.

"Who wouldn't be?" Harry said in a steady cool voice. "It's a bad storm."

Peter took his key from the string around his neck,

opened the chest, and pulled out a candle and matches. He lit the candle and set it in an empty sardine tin. Light from the candle showed Harry's face more clearly. His eyes were red as though he'd been crying. It made Peter want to blow the candle out again.

"Why were you out in the storm?" Peter asked. He pulled off his rain slicker, folded it, and put it in the corner, off the carpeting.

"I like to walk in the rain," Harry said stiffly. "It's good for your health."

"I don't blame you for not wanting to tell me. I've not been very kind to you since you moved here."

"You didn't squeal on me at the party last night."

"You knew that I saw you?"

Harry nodded. As he turned his head, the flickering candlelight showed red marks on his neck.

"I kept the secret last night. I'll keep this one, too. What happened to you?"

Harry was quiet. His lower lip quivered. Peter was afraid the boy was going to cry again. Then Harry whispered, "Father."

"Your father hurt you?" Peter was incredulous.

Harry nodded.

"Why?"

"Drunk."

Peter sat very still, trying to grasp this truth. It seemed so impossible. No father could treat a son like this.

"He doesn't know what he's doing," Harry added lamely. "Sometimes he doesn't even remember what he does or what he says." He paused. "And he can say some terrible things."

"So you ran off?"

Harry shook his head. "He locked me out."

Peter couldn't help it. He gasped, and the sound filled the clubhouse. Rags whined and scooted closer to Peter.

"Can't you climb back in a window or something?"

"I'd just as soon not try it." He rubbed at the red place on his neck. "I can wait until he's sober. This isn't the first time."

"You've come to the clubhouse before?"

Harry gave a weak smile. "It's been very handy. Good thing Avery doesn't know, huh?"

Peter ignored the reference to Avery. He'd never really agreed with the way Avery attacked Harry, and yet he'd never done much about it. In a way, he was as guilty as Avery.

"You don't have to tell me this if you don't want to," Peter said, "but did Mattie really fall off your back porch?"

Harry shook his head, his eyes brimming with tears.

"Your father did that, too?"

The tears spilled over onto Harry's cheeks. He wiped them with the back of his fist. "I hate him when he's like that. But what can I do? He's so much bigger. If I were a man, I'd take Mama and Mattie and go where he'd never find us."

Peter remembered how bad Mattie's face had looked, and he shivered.

"He promised when we received the inheritance from Mama's uncle that he would change. 'I'm a new man,' he told us. But nothing changed. I believe Father was drunk when he bought the house in this neighborhood. Even with the inheritance money, we can't afford anything like this.

It's insane. Now the business is going sour. I don't know how much more we can take."

"I won't tell," Peter promised. "I won't tell anyone."

"Thanks."

"Except. . ."

"Except what?" Harry swiped at his cheek again with his shirt sleeve.

"There's someone I know who could help."

Harry shook his head. "No one can help. There's nothing anyone can do."

"My aunt understands all about this. She works with. . ." Peter stopped.

"It's all right. I know Papa's a drunkard. You can say it."

"Anyway, she knows and she understands. Will you go with me to her house?"

The rain was pattering down gently, and the wind had stopped blowing.

"Who's your aunt?"

"Elise Stevenson. My uncle Abe was the one with the magic lantern show last night. They won't tell anyone. I know they won't."

"I watched him playing with the other kids," Harry said. "Your uncle seems like a nice man."

"He's the swellest man you ever met," Peter assured him. "Come on." Peter stood, picked up his slicker, and blew out the candle. "You can get under here with me." He stepped outside into the light rain and lifted the slicker so Harry could get under with him. Together they walked the few blocks to Uncle Abe's house, with Rags trailing behind.

Uncle Abe and Aunt Elise were up because of the storm. "Peter!" Aunt Elise said when she opened the door. "Your mama just telephoned to see if we'd seen you." Looking at Harry, she said, "Well, well. Who have we here?"

"Aunt Elise, this is Harry Dawes. He has a real bad problem. I told him I thought you and Uncle Abe could help."

"Did I hear my name?" Uncle Abe came up behind his wife.

"The boys are wet," Aunt Elise said, ushering the two inside. "We'll have Carleen make hot spiced tea."

"Stay," Peter said to Rags, who obediently curled up on the hall rug. He seemed quite happy to have been rescued—again.

Peter used Aunt Elise's telephone to call Mama. He told her he'd found Rags in the clubhouse and that he'd come to Aunt Elise's to get dry before coming home.

Harry and Peter then sat in the blue breakfast nook with Uncle Abe and Aunt Elise. Harry told his story once again. Aunt Elise was filled with compassion for him, just as Peter knew she would be.

"There's not much we can do just now," Aunt Elise said, "but we can do a little. First of all, this will be your place of safety. If you and Mattie need to get away, you come here."

Harry nodded and blinked back tears.

"But more importantly," she continued, "now that we know the problem, we can be praying for your father. The Lord wants to set him free from this terrible enslavement. Down at the mission where I volunteer, we see men being set free every day."

Peter trusted that her words gave Harry a glimmer of hope. How awful it would be to be frightened of your own father.

Just then, Aunt Elise told Peter he'd better get on home.

"You did the right thing bringing your friend to us," she said. "We'll let him sleep here tonight."

As Peter and Rags walked slowly toward home, he remembered what Allyson had said about being glad no drunk lived in their neighborhood. But now he knew—a drunk really did live in their neighborhood.

It explained a lot about why Harry acted like he did. No wonder he stayed off by himself. Peter stopped in the clubhouse and returned the candle, the matches, and the sardine tin to the chest. He didn't want either Avery or Heber to know anyone had been in there.

The clouds were breaking up, and a few stars glittered in the velvet sky. As he came to their back door, Peter leaned down to pet Rags. "I guess since the screen has a hole in it, I'll just have to take you up to my bedroom," he whispered.

He hung his slicker on the hall tree so it could dry, then scooped Rags up in his arms and went up the stairs.

"I'm sorry you ran away, Rags," he whispered. "But I'm sure glad you led me to Harry." Then he remembered something. "You know, Rags, Aunt Elise called Harry my friend."

He put Rags down on the chenille rug beside his bed. "Maybe he is, Rags. Maybe he is."

CHAPTER 12
The Fastest Runner

The Fourth of July meant a huge picnic in Central Park with food, music, games, and fireworks. Peter could hardly wait. Other than going to the cabin at Bear Claw Lake in August, the Fourth of July was his favorite part of summer.

Mr. Kingsbury asked that he work a couple hours early in the day. "Just until we get all the rented surreys and carriages out of here," he said.

By the time Peter went home to change clothes and walked with Rags to the park, it looked as though every inhabitant of Fair Oaks was there. The park was a beehive of activity. One-legged races and sack races were going on. Near the lemonade stand, a pie-eating contest was in progress. Several high school boys were eating blackberry pies with their hands tied behind their backs. Their faces were smeared with purple, and the crowd roared with laughter.

"There you are!" Avery came running up to him, with Heber right behind.

"We've been waiting for you," Heber said. "Now we can have some real fun."

"Come with us to the track on the far side of the lake," Avery said. "I'm going to be in the bicycle race."

The three boys ran through the crowds with Rags at their heels. The bicycle race was conducted on an oval track near Johnson Lake. Entrants were selected according to age, which meant that Avery would compete against four other boys his age. Heber and Peter cheered until they were hoarse, and Rags barked as though it were his contribution to the cheering section. To their delight, Avery won quite handily.

"Next year, I'll be in that race with my bicycle," Peter said to Heber.

His friend smiled. "I bet I'll have my bicycle then, too. Won't we have fun when all three of us are riding our bicycles together all over the neighborhood?"

Next, it was time for the high-wheelers to race. These bicycles, ridden by adults, had high front wheels. They were dangerous and made for great sport. The crowd went wild with cheering for their favorite entrants.

While everyone was focused on the race, Peter happened to see a family standing at the fringes of the crowd. It was Mr. and Mrs. Dawes with Harry and Mattie. Peter tried not to stare. By all appearances, they looked like a happy family, no different than anyone else in the crowd.

Mr. Dawes was a tall, raw-boned man with hands that looked too big for his body. He was wearing a straw boater and a stylish pale linen suit. He smiled beneath his handlebar mustache as he tipped his hat politely to passersby.

His wife, whom Peter had only seen from a distance, was thin and mousey looking. Her long dark skirt had no bustle, and her hat sported only a few silk flowers, unlike the grand creations worn by all the other ladies.

At one point Harry happened to look Peter's way. Their eyes met. Peter gave a quick nod. Harry nodded back. But that was all.

After the bicycle races, the boys rode the swan boats across the lake, fussing over who got to work the pedals first. The sun was hot, making the breeze off the lake even more refreshing. Rags sat on the seat beside Peter and barked as other boats passed them on the glassy water.

As they were returning to the dock, Avery pulled out his silver watch. "We're just in time for the foot races. Let's all enter."

"Aw, go on," Heber said. "You know I'm no good at running."

It was true. Heber became winded just paddling the swan boat.

"It doesn't matter," Avery said. "Let's all enter as members of the Shady Vinewood Club."

"All for one," Peter said.

"And one for all," Avery finished, giving Heber a hand up out of the swan boat.

"Oh, all right," Heber said. "But promise you won't laugh when I come in last."

"Shady Vinewood Club members do not laugh at one another," Peter said in a somber tone.

"And besides," Avery added, "it's for the fun of the race, not for the winning."

The younger boys raced first. A section of the bicycle track had been designated for the foot races. Men with stopwatches were stationed, two at the starting point, two at the finish line. When the first race was completed, they announced the race for ages ten through twelve.

"That's us," Avery said.

Peter handed Rags over to Carol, who was at the sidelines. The Shady Vinewood Club members ran toward the starting point and lined up at the mark. Almost a dozen boys entered the race. Peter knew the competition would be stiff.

Just then, Harry came to the edge of the track, sat down, and removed his shoes and stockings. He handed them to Mattie and came to the starting point standing, beside Peter.

"What's the hayseed doing here?" Avery growled.

"Running a race," Peter answered. "Just like we are."

"He doesn't belong here." Avery's voice was low, but Peter knew Harry heard every word.

"I guess he has as much right to be in the race as we do," Peter said.

Just then one of the men held up a red handkerchief. "On the word *go,*" he told them, "I'll bring the handkerchief down. That's your signal for the race to begin. Everyone ready?"

Peter held his breath, fearing Avery would make a scene about Harry being a part of the race. Thankfully he didn't.

The man yelled out, "On your mark. Get set. Go!" The red handkerchief came down, and the boys took off. Peter tried to

101

keep his mind on the finish line. He knew his long legs were as fast or faster than anyone there. Suddenly Harry came pressing up behind him and easily passed him. Avery was just behind Peter. He whispered, "Trip him, Peter. Trip him."

Peter pushed into a last burst of speed and acted as though he'd never heard. He and Harry were in a dead heat as they rounded the corner at one end of the track and headed toward the finish line.

It was as though Harry had saved a bit of energy for the very last part of the race. Suddenly he sprinted across the finish line, a good three feet ahead of Peter. Peter had never so enjoyed losing a race in his life. He went right up to Harry and shook his hand and slapped his shoulder.

Then the Dawes family was there. Mattie was carrying Harry's shoes and was squealing with excitement. Mrs. Dawes was smiling, and Mr. Dawes came up and put his big hand on Harry's shoulder and said something that made the boy smile.

Peter was watching the scene unfold when suddenly an angry Avery was at his side. "You could have stopped him," he muttered.

"I could have," Peter said, "but somehow that doesn't seem very fair."

Heber came up beside them puffing and blowing. "Did Peter win?" he asked.

Avery didn't bother to hide his disgust. "He let the hayseed win."

"Peter did?" Heber looked at Peter with a blank expression.

"You know better than that, Heber. I didn't *let* him—he won it fair and square. Even barefooted, he's faster than I am."

Avery was bristling with anger. "That's not all, Heber." He spit the words out. "He actually shook his hand and congratulated him."

Heber's face was flushed and streaked with perspiration. He pulled out his shirttail, wiped his face with the corner, then hurriedly tucked it in before anyone saw him. "Why'd you do that, Peter?"

"Because he won, silly." To Avery he said, "Didn't you just tell Heber this was all for the fun of the race? Now what say let's go get some iced lemonade?"

For the rest of the day, Avery was out of sorts. Once when he rode off with two other boys on their bicycles, Heber said to Peter, "I wish you hadn't made Avery mad. I don't like it when he's mad. He may take the wooden chest back and not let us wear our keys."

"I don't think he'd do that, Heber," Peter said. "He likes the club too much to break it up."

Quite honestly, Peter wasn't sure what Avery might do. Even though he tried to act as though it didn't bother him, he had to admit it was awful to have Avery so upset. It made him feel sick.

When the family walked toward home that evening, they discussed all the wonderful events of the day. Carol and Odele had won the three-legged race. Of course, they'd been secretly practicing for weeks.

As they approached their house, Carol said, "That Harry Dawes sure is a good runner."

"He sure is," Peter agreed. "And he runs barefooted."

"I'm truly glad he won."

Peter didn't answer, but deep down, he felt the same way.

CHAPTER 13

To Bear Claw Lake

Throughout the hot summer days, Peter loved going to work at the livery. He quickly learned the personalities of each of the horses. Mr. Kingsbury complimented him by saying he had a way with the horses. At first Peter was only allowed to clean stalls, spread clean straw, and fill the feed bunks. Later he was trusted to mix feed and groom and harness the horses.

On Sundays at Grandpa's house after church, Grandpa would ask Peter about his work and Peter would report something new he'd learned. The whole family seemed proud of his achievements. Peter could barely remember that he'd been upset at Grandpa's challenge at first. The coins in his tin were accumulating nicely.

One sticky July day he was walking home from work with Rags trotting along beside him, when Carol came skipping rope down the sidewalk toward him.

"Hi, Peter," she said. Folding up her red-handled skip rope, she fell into step beside him, stopping just a moment to pat Rags's head.

"Hi," Peter answered. "How come you're not playing with Odele and Mattie?"

Carol shrugged. "It's kinda hot."

Peter didn't mention she'd just been skipping rope in that heat.

She gave a little giggle. "You smell like horses."

"I like the smell of horses," he replied.

"I do, too. When it's on the horse."

Peter laughed at her joke. But then she turned serious. "Peter, do you think something is wrong at the Daweses' house?"

Peter wasn't sure how to answer that. "What do you mean, wrong?"

"I don't know exactly. I don't think they have very much money. Mattie's been wearing the same smock and pinafore over and over again. Sometimes it gets pretty dirty before it gets washed."

"What else?"

Carol stopped walking. Tears formed in her eyes. "Peter, today Mattie told me she was hungry."

"What's wrong with that? Everyone gets hungry." Peter had a hunch what she was getting at, but something inside him didn't want to hear it.

"She begged me not to tell anyone, but there's no food in their house." Carol twisted the skip rope in her hands.

"No food. Can you imagine that?"

Peter couldn't imagine that. No more than he could imagine being locked out of the house on a stormy night. He knew Carol wasn't really looking for an answer. She just needed to talk to someone. "What did you do?" he asked.

"I took her to our house and asked Stella to let us have a snack. Then I gave her all mine."

"That was kind of you."

She started walking again. "It wasn't much. I wish we could do more. Why don't they have food, Peter? Mr. Dawes owns a business. Why don't they have any food?"

Peter considered telling Carol what he knew, but thought better of it. After all, he'd promised Harry he wouldn't tell. "Maybe the business isn't doing well," he told her. "But I think I know a way to help."

"Oh, Peter," Carol said. "I knew you would. Tell me what you plan to do."

"I'll tell you if it works."

In his room, Peter poured water into the china washbowl from the flowered pitcher and washed his hands and face, then changed clothes. He folded his soiled work clothes over the clothes rack at the foot of the bed.

Then he got out the money tin. There wasn't a penny to spare, but this was an emergency. He removed two dollars' worth of coins and put them in his pocket. After lunch, instead of going to the vacant lot to find Heber and Avery, he walked toward town and went to the corner grocery market.

"Hello there, Peter," the owner, Mr. Schoch, greeted him. "Your mother usually telephones your grocery orders. Did she forget something this week?"

Peter's mind was racing. "I'm running an errand for

Mrs. Dawes," he said. "She'd like a few things delivered this afternoon."

"Good for you, Peter. Helping around the neighborhood, are you?" Mr. Schoch took the stub of a pencil from behind his ear and pulled out his order pad. "What will it be?"

"Huh?"

"What does Mrs. Dawes want? Didn't she send you with a list?"

Peter could have kicked himself. He should have made a list. He'd never shopped for groceries before. He didn't have much of an idea what women needed in the kitchen. "I have it all memorized," he said touching his finger to his brow. "Now let's see how well I do."

He looked about the shelves. He didn't even know if he had enough money. "A loaf of bread," he said. That would be a good start. They could make sandwiches if they had bread. "A pound of sliced bologna." Peter loved bologna sandwiches with lettuce. "A head of lettuce," he added. Looking at the pickle barrel, he said, "Three dill pickles."

Mr. Schoch continued to write as Peter gave the order. He added in apples and bananas and two tins of sardines. Then he thought of cans of soup and crackers from the cracker barrel. "How much does that come to?" he asked.

The pencil made scratching noises on the order pad. "Exactly one dollar and ninety-five cents."

Peter fished in his pockets. "She sent the money with me."

"Oh good," Mr. Schoch replied. "Their credit is getting a little shaky around here."

Together they counted out the right amount. Peter put the remaining nickel back in his pocket. "Max will be back with the wagon in a few minutes," Mr. Schoch said. "We'll get this delivered to Mrs. Dawes within the hour." Max was Mr. Schoch's sixteen-year-old son.

"Thank you," Peter said as he left to go home.

Later he hid across the street from the Daweses' house and watched as the dray pulled up with *Schoch Cash Grocery* painted on the side. He could hear Mrs. Dawes's flustered voice trying to argue with Max Schoch, but in the end, the groceries were carried into Mrs. Dawes's house in a pasteboard box.

When Peter arrived late at the clubhouse, Avery and Heber demanded to know where he'd been. All he would say was that he'd had an errand to run.

That night as he lay in bed, he struggled as he thought of the money that was now missing from the tin box. But then he thought of Mattie and Harry and Mrs. Dawes eating bologna sandwiches with lettuce, and he slept.

When Peter first hired on at Kingsbury Livery, he had informed Mr. Kingsbury about the two weeks in August when he would be gone to Bear Claw Lake. "We go every summer," Peter told him.

As August drew nearer, Mr. Kingsbury began to tease him about not wanting to let him go. "When we first made the agreement, I didn't know how good an employee you would be," he said. "Now that you've become so good at your work, I can't afford to let you go."

His praise made Peter feel ten feet tall. He knew he'd miss all the horses. And he'd also miss Albert and Jerry. They'd all had good times together. Sometimes they had water fights, and Peter and Albert had a few wrestling matches in the hay. But all was in good fun, and Mr. Kingsbury tolerated the nonsense as long as it didn't disrupt the business. Which it never did.

But by the time Mama began packing the big trunks to go to the lake, Peter felt the old excitement rising up. In the woods around the lake it was always cooler than in the city. And there were ever so many wonderful things to do. He and Avery and Heber talked of how they could continue their club meetings at the lake.

"And," Avery added, "won't it be good to get away from that Harry Dawes? I see him snooping around the vacant lot every once in awhile. I hope he's not been snooping in our clubhouse."

Peter bit his tongue as he thought of the times Harry had used the little lean-to as his getaway shelter.

When it came time to take the bags and trunks to the train station, Father used the Kingsbury Livery. Peter knew the teams of horses by name. When they nickered in recognition of his voice, Allyson was duly impressed.

"They act like they really know you," she said.

"Of course they know me. Just like Rags knows me," he said.

Rags was whining his displeasure at being boxed up in a wooden crate with slats in the sides. His place on the train would be the baggage car. The man at the train station had told Peter he could go to the baggage car at any time during the trip and check on his dog.

Peter sat with Albert Kingsbury in the front of the wagon loaded with all their things. The other members of the family followed in a carriage. It was Friday afternoon, the last day of July. Father would stay with them at the lake for the weekend, then return to the city on Monday for work.

At the station platform, there was a great deal of dashing about, calling out orders, and general unorganized confusion. Everyone was full of eager anticipation. Many Fair Oaks families made this summer outing a seasonal tradition. The adults gave last-minute instructions to the drivers, while at the same time they tried to keep overexcited children in tow.

Avery and Heber were there with their families, and both boys were all smiles. As usual, Martin was giving Naomi meaningful looks, and as usual, Naomi was giggling. Avery had told Peter and Heber that the only good thing about Naomi's new interest in Martin was that she was too distracted to be a bossy tattletale.

The train whistle blew in the distance. Within minutes the giant puffing locomotive was chugging to a stop, and passengers began debarking.

Peter stayed with Albert and helped to transfer baggage from the wagon to the train. That way he was able to see right where Rags's crate was placed. He made sure the metal water dish was firmly fastened to the side. Then he said good-bye to Albert and joined his family in the coach.

Mama allowed Peter to sit with Avery and Heber. They talked the entire way about the fish they would catch and the arrowheads they would find and their own little secret island. Of course it wasn't really a secret, but it was a great place to get away from the others. It also was close enough to shore so that their parents allowed them to take the rowboat out to it.

Some of the families stayed in the big three-story stone lodge with its wide veranda. But Peter's family had a cabin that was really larger than a cabin. The word *cabin* always made Peter think of a one-room log cabin like the one where

110

Abraham Lincoln was born. But their cabin at the lake had a nice upstairs, plenty of airy bedrooms, and a big screened-in back porch where they played on rainy afternoons.

The train station at Bear Claw Lodge was much smaller than the one in Minneapolis, but there were wagons and carriages waiting to take them to their cabins.

By nightfall, the Morgans were almost all settled in. Back home, Father hardly ever set foot in the kitchen. But at the lake, the rules somehow changed, and he enjoyed helping Mama and Stella arrange the foodstuffs and supplies in the cupboards and pantry.

Peter decided to keep Rags on a rope attached to his collar for the first day or so. After all, there were wild animals out in the woods. If he ran away here, he could really get hurt.

The first evening, Heber, Avery, and Peter sat out on the fishing dock and watched a scarlet sunset reflect on the rippling surface of the water. They were soaking up the fresh country air and thinking.

After a time, Avery spoke. "Peter, are you hoping you'll have another baby brother so there won't be any more girls in your family?"

Peter stopped staring at the red ball of sun that was setting down gently on the thick pines across the lake. He turned to Avery. "What? Baby brother? What are you talking about?"

Avery laughed. "Don't tell me you don't know. My mama told me there's going to be another little Morgan coming along this year." He slapped Heber on the shoulder. "Just think, Hebe. His own mama. And he doesn't even know."

"Well, what do you know about that?" Peter said.

CHAPTER 14

Uncle Abe Brings a Surprise

Having Rags at the lake made a wonderful time even better. Mama didn't care that Peter slept out on the screened-in porch and that Rags crawled right onto the cot with him. Every night Peter fell asleep listening to the frogs and crickets singing out in the dense woods. It was heavenly.

The boys ran and played from sunup until sundown. They took turns rowing the rowboat. Some days they took picnic lunches to the island. On those days, the parents insisted that Odele, Carol, and Allyson be allowed to go along.

Fish were snagged, cleaned, and fried for supper. Heber found new arrowheads to add to his collection. Once they happened to catch Martin kissing Naomi. It made Naomi furious, which made the boys laugh even harder.

In the backyard of the Norton cabin, Avery's father had set up a croquet game. Even the mothers came out to play croquet in the cool evening air.

One evening, as Peter and Carol sat talking on the back porch, he asked her if she knew there was to be another baby in the family. Carol smiled. "We girls know those kinds of things," she said.

Peter marveled. He guessed he hadn't paid much attention. Mama had always been a little on the plump side. She didn't have a waspish waist like Miss Minor. But sure enough, the next time Peter took a good look, Mama's tummy did seem bigger than usual.

Carol said the baby would be born around Christmas. "Wouldn't you know," she added. "Another one to have to struggle with a holiday birthday—and another one for me to have to share a birthday with."

Peter could tell she wasn't too happy about the matter.

Aunt Elise and Uncle Abe had not come with the rest of them because of other things they had to do. But they were scheduled to arrive that Friday evening. Father was to arrive at the same time, returning for yet another weekend.

Peter, Carol, and Allyson were excited. Uncle Abe was always so much fun, but they also hoped he would bring along his magic lantern. And he did. But he and Aunt Elise also brought another surprise.

Peter, Avery, and Heber had been digging in the rocky beach all afternoon, creating miniature lakes and rivers on the shore. They had come back to the cabins to wait for the arriving family members.

As the carriages pulled up in front of the cabins, there,

sitting right between Aunt Elise and Uncle Abe was Harry Dawes!

Avery's jaw immediately tightened. "What's *he* doing here?" he demanded so only Peter and Heber could hear. Looking right at Peter, he said, "Why did *your* uncle have to bring *him* here?"

Peter was as surprised as the rest. "I have no idea," he said. Peter had planned to run right up to Uncle Abe and Aunt Elise and hug them and welcome them. But now he didn't know what to do.

Harry's presence had no effect on Odele, Carol, and Allyson. They ran to meet the carriage and swarmed all over the new arrivals. Though Peter hated to do it, he hung back with Heber and Avery.

When Harry looked their way, Peter acted as though he didn't see. "Come on, guys. We'll let Uncle Abe and Aunt Elise get settled in. We can always talk to them later."

The entire vacation had changed. They had been having so much fun. Now it was spoiled.

Later that evening Peter learned from Father that Uncle Abe had been taking Harry to the YMCA once a week and the two had become good friends.

That night as Peter lay on his cot on the porch, with Rags snuggled in right beside him, he wrestled with the problem. What must Uncle Abe think of him for keeping his distance? Part of him wanted very much to pull Harry right into all their fun. But on the other hand, he didn't want to make Avery mad. After all, he and Avery had been friends as long as he could remember. And what about the club? The Shady Vinewood Club was important to Peter, and he didn't want to lose it.

He reached up to touch the brass key hanging from the string around his neck. The only time he ever took it off was to unlock the chest. He even wore it in the bathtub.

Why did Uncle Abe have to befriend Harry anyway? Then the realization hit Peter like a bucket of ice water—*he* was the one who'd introduced the two in the first place. What would Avery think if he knew that?

Peter let out a groan, and it made Rags whine and lick Peter's hand. "What am I going to do, Rags? This mess is ruining the most wonderful two weeks of the entire year." But Rags had no answer. Unfortunately, Peter didn't either.

Harry wore his overalls every day. Sometimes with no shirt. It looked cool and comfortable. Peter wished he'd brought his dungarees. He could have rolled up the legs. But Mama only packed his cotton play clothes.

Avery's plan was to pretend that Harry didn't exist. However, that was rather difficult. The boy seemed to be more at home in the woods than anyone else there. He was always popping out of the strangest places. And most amazing of all, Harry could swim. Although the other boys came to the lake every summer, they had never been allowed to go swimming. The parents all agreed that it was too dangerous. But Harry just ran to the end of the dock and dived in head first. Peter stared dumbfounded.

"Don't look," Avery ordered. "He's just showing off."

"Looks like he's just having fun to me," Heber said.

"Well then," Avery said curtly, "why don't you go have fun with him?"

"I didn't say I wanted to have fun with him," Heber countered. "I just said it looks like—"

"I know what you said," Avery snapped. "Now are we going to play or just stand around gawking like a bunch of dummies?"

Avery led the way into the woods behind the cabins. They walked beside a creek that fed into the lake. In places it was shallow enough for wading. Other spots were deep and full of whirling eddies that looked spooky and dangerous. Throwing sticks into the eddies was great fun. The boys watched them whirl about and then get sucked down into the deep pool. By suppertime, they'd almost forgotten that Harry Dawes existed.

But hard as he tried, Peter simply could not ignore the boy's presence. Carleen, Aunt Elise's cook, had come with them, and her little daughter, Maureen, could often be seen playing in the backyard of the Stevenson cabin. A couple times, Peter saw Harry back there swinging Maureen in the glider swing. Peter wondered how a boy who spent time with a toddler could be so bad. He'd heard Aunt Elise tell Mama that Harry was ever so much help around the cabin, willing to do most anything that needed done.

Peter, on the other hand, didn't spend that much time with his own baby brother. In fact, Mark could be a pain, getting into things all the time and setting up a wail whenever Peter made him get out of his stuff.

On Monday, Uncle Abe didn't go back to the city with the other men. He was taking the whole week off. One afternoon, he took Peter aside and asked him about Harry. "You were the one who was so concerned about him the night of the storm," Uncle Abe said. "I thought sure if I brought him here to the lake, you'd make him feel welcome. I guess I was wrong."

Uncle Abe's words hurt something fierce. Peter tried to

explain what good friends Avery and Heber were, but even as he said it, he knew he had no defense. Thankfully, Uncle Abe didn't argue the point.

Nothing, absolutely nothing was making any sense. Avery was upset most of the time. He made no bones about blaming Peter, since it was Peter's uncle who'd brought Harry. Peter found himself wishing he were back home working in the livery stable. He was always happy there.

Avery and Heber had their fishing poles out one afternoon and were planning to fish off the dock. Peter told them to go ahead, that he would join them later. Instead, he took Rags and headed up into the wooded hills to be alone. He just needed to think and sort things out.

It was a glorious day with the sun breaking through the thick stands of pines. The aroma of spicy pine filled the air. Peter found a stick to use for Rags to play fetch. Each time the dog came bounding back with the stick in his mouth, Peter gave him a hug, ruffled his soft fur, and kissed the top of his head. "You're such a good dog, Rags. I love you, boy."

They played for a time, then Peter sat against a tree on the creek bank and watched the water rushing by. He knew Avery and Heber were probably wondering where he was, but he didn't really care. After all, didn't he have a right to be by himself if he wanted? It had become tiresome to be with Avery when all he did was talk bad about Harry and blame Peter.

The stillness of the woods made him sleepy, and he leaned back against the tree and closed his eyes. His mind went to the Sunday school lesson about the Good Samaritan. He wondered again about that strange man. Would the man have stopped to help if other Samaritans had been with him?

What if they had been saying, "Don't touch him. Remember, we're supposed to hate the Jews"?

Peter recalled how Miss Chenoweth explained that the Samaritan not only tended to the wounds of the man, but put him on his donkey and paid for him to stay at the inn. That's a lot of good things to do for someone you're supposed to hate.

Suddenly, Rags's barking jolted him upright. A cottontail rabbit had bounded out of the woods. Peter laughed at the sight. He didn't know who was the most surprised, the dog or the rabbit. Rags jumped up and took off like a streak, right on the heels of that cottontail.

Peter called for him to come back, but the dog was too agitated. Just then the rabbit zigzagged, throwing the dog off, and Rags went flying right into the creek. Peter stood to his feet and ran toward the spot. He wasn't too concerned. Rags often jumped off the dock into the lake to cool off and came paddling easily back to shore. But then Peter saw something that made him freeze with fear. The whirling eddy!

CHAPTER 15

A New Friend

Peter watched in sheer terror as the current pulled Rags closer to the eddy. Tears ran down his cheeks. "No, Rags. No! Please!" he yelled. "Somebody help! Please help!"

In a flash, Harry Dawes ran past him, pulling off his shirt as he came. Peter caught his arm. "No, Harry. The eddy."

"Find a long branch," he said and dove in.

Peter watched for a moment as Harry swam in bold strong strokes toward the floundering dog. Peter shook himself and then ran to find the largest branch he could carry. He ran back to the creek bank, getting as close as he could.

Harry had his arm around Rags and was pulling himself and the dog toward the bank just a few feet shy of the swirling eddy. Peter pushed the large limb into the water and held the other end with all his might. He could not breathe as he watched Harry struggling to catch hold.

Harry grasped the limb twice, but the current pulled him away. Finally he had an arm over the branch and hung there for a moment to catch his breath.

"Come as close as you can," Harry said between gasps. "I'm going to give Rags a hard shove toward you. Reach out and grab him."

"Be careful," Peter told him.

Doing as he said, Harry gave Rags a hard shove, using all his strength. The momentum sent Rags toward the bank. Peter reached out and grabbed the dog's foreleg and dragged him up on the bank. But the force of the shove made Harry lose his grip, and he was again fighting the current. This time both of his strong arms were free.

Peter had never felt so helpless. He turned his back on Rags, who was lying on the thick pine needles, panting and whimpering. He moved down the bank as fast as he could, carrying the large branch, and positioned himself ahead of where the current was carrying Harry.

"Here," he called out. "Grab the limb." Peter stretched across one end of the limb, putting his full weight on it to hold it steady. Fighting the strong current, Harry moved toward the limb and made it. Peter reached out as far as he could to grasp Harry's hand. Within a few moments Harry was up and out of the water. For a moment they just lay on the grassy bank with Harry gasping for air.

"The dog?" Harry asked when he could speak.

Peter pointed over at Rags, who was on his feet and walking toward them. "Fine," he said. "Just fine."

Rags came closer and then stopped and shook himself from the top of his head to the very tip of his tail, sending a spray of creek water over both of them. Suddenly they were laughing. Laughing at Rags. Laughing for sheer relief. Just laughing for no reason. It was the first time Peter had ever heard Harry Dawes laugh.

They sat there for awhile. Peter tried to grasp what had just happened. Harry had risked his life for Rags. It was almost too big a thought to grasp. Especially after the terrible way he'd treated Harry. In Peter's mind, this was a genuine Good Samaritan act.

Peter didn't know what to say. He didn't know where to begin. All he could muster up was a weak "Thank you." There was no way he could ever thank Harry enough. What he did say was, "I sure wish I could swim like you."

"We had a pond on a farm where we lived a few years ago. I snuck off and learned on my own. It's not hard to learn." Harry pulled on his shirt and let it hang open over his wet overalls. "I could probably teach you."

"Really?"

"Sure."

Rags lay down and put his face in Harry's lap. He looked up with his soft brown eyes. Harry smiled and gently stroked the wet fur. "Good boy," he said. "Such a good dog." Any other time, Peter would have been jealous, but he knew this was Rags's way of saying thank you.

Harry stood. "I guess I'd better be getting on back. Your aunt will be wondering where I am." He paused a moment. "You don't have to walk back with me if you don't want to.

I know your friend Avery doesn't like me."

"No!" Peter didn't want to hear Harry talk like that. He jumped up as well. "What I mean is, let's walk back together. I *want* to walk back with you."

"Okay."

And they did. As they walked along, Harry pointed out a place where a deer had rubbed his antlers on a tree trunk and noted the trail of a badger on the ground.

"You know a lot about the woods," Peter said.

Harry nodded. "I'm more at home in the woods than in a big city like Minneapolis."

Presently they emerged from the woods into the clearing down a ways from the row of cabins. Heber and Avery were walking along the lakeshore, carrying their poles and a can of worms. When they saw Peter and Harry, the other two boys stopped and stared as though they couldn't believe what they were seeing. Peter felt Harry hesitate beside him, but Peter kept right on walking toward the duo. Harry followed.

"Where've you been?" Heber demanded. "We've been looking everywhere for you."

"Heber, Avery," Peter said, "I've decided I'd like for Harry to be included in the things we do. Things like our games and fishing and boating and arrowhead hunting."

"Just here?" Heber said. "You mean just at the lake?"

Peter knew what he was getting at. It might be okay to be friends with Harry at the lake but then ignore him back at Fair Oaks. "No, not just at the lake."

"Over my dead body," Avery said through clenched teeth. "The Shady Vinewood Club is not open to new members."

Peter took a deep breath. He knew what he had to do. Reaching for the string around his neck, he carefully lifted it over his head. Heber's eyes grew wide as he watched.

"Here," Peter said, handing the brass key to Avery. "Here's my key. If our club means we have to be unkind, then I guess I'd rather not be a member."

"Don't do that," Heber said, his voice quivering. "You're ruining everything."

Avery reached over and elbowed Heber. "Let him go, Heber. We don't need him. You and I'll have the best club ever. In fact," Avery added as he put his arm about Heber's shoulder, "as soon as we get home, I'm going to let you ride my bicycle any time you want."

"Any time?" Heber said, his voice going a little squeaky.

"Any time."

Peter watched as the two walked away with their arms slung over one another's shoulders. His two best friends were walking away. Strange as it seemed, he didn't feel bad. He looked over at Harry and smiled.

"I'm sorry," Harry said.

Peter knelt down and put his arms around Rags's neck. "Don't be sorry, Harry. I'm not. I'm not sorry one bit."

The rest of the week, Harry taught Peter how to track deer and tell different kinds of trees by the shapes of their leaves. He showed Peter how to find his way out of the woods if he ever get lost. Then the two of them stole away to a place far down the lake where Harry taught Peter how to swim. Peter couldn't remember ever having so much fun at the lake. Not even a bicycle was this much fun.

One afternoon when Aunt Elise was at their cabin, she put her arm around Peter's shoulder. "We're so proud of you, Peter," she said. "Harry needed a friend like you."

Peter smiled. "Maybe I needed a friend like him."

Aunt Elise patted his shoulder and chuckled. "You're probably right!"

The last night at the lake, Uncle Abe hung a bedsheet in the trees out behind his cabin and invited all the families for a magic lantern show. There was lemonade and watermelon and homemade ice cream and cake. Harry and Peter were put to work cranking the ice cream freezers. They cranked till their arms were aching.

Avery and Heber stayed off to the side as though they weren't sure they wanted to be part of what Uncle Abe was doing, and yet they wanted to see the show. Peter paid them scant attention. He knew he'd done the right thing.

They'd been back in the city only a few days when Carol learned from Mattie that the Dawes family was once again out of food.

"Can you perform another miracle?" she asked Peter.

"I think I can," he said. But Peter didn't want to take the chance of pretending he was running errands for Mrs. Dawes. He might get caught. Now more than ever, he didn't want to do anything that would embarrass Harry.

Now that Peter was no longer a club member, he didn't have to hurry to the clubhouse each afternoon. So the next day when he was off work, he walked to a corner grocery where no one knew him. He bought a basket of groceries and paid for it with his bicycle money and then hid the basket in the toolshed behind their house until after dark.

Ever since they'd returned from the lake, Peter had been sleeping on the sunporch because of the heat. That made it easy to slip out in the night, sneak over to the Daweses' house, and leave the basket on the back porch. How Peter wished he were a millionaire like Avery's father. He'd feed all the hungry children in the whole city.

Peter stayed away from the clubhouse on Shady Lane. He and Harry played together at Central Park, especially in the area around Lake Johnson. Of course it was just a little pond compared to Bear Claw Lake, but Harry said it was like having a little bit of country in the city. They caught frogs and hunted for turtles, and sometimes they even saw a rabbit or two.

One afternoon Aunt Elise let Harry and Peter ride her bicycle in the privacy of her backyard. It was great fun. And Harry learned to ride almost immediately.

Summer was winding down, and the first day of school was drawing closer. This would be Allyson's first year at Fair Oaks, and she could hardly wait.

One day Harry told Peter, "I don't think I'll go back to school this year. I may just quit."

"Why?" Peter said. "Don't you know how important it is to get an education?"

Peter had heard that all his life so he guessed it was true. They were sitting on the edge of Johnson Lake. Each boy had a long stick that they were dragging back and forth through the water. Rags was stretched out in the grass between them with his pink tongue hanging out.

"I'm going to get a job," Harry said. "If I get a job and work hard, I'll be like Tattered Tom in the Horatio Alger novel—someday I'll be a successful businessman."

"Is it because the other kids tease you about your clothes? Is that why you don't want to go?"

Harry nodded. "You're pretty smart."

125

"I don't think the other kids care that much. Avery's the only one who harped about it. Why let one boy ruin your chance for an education?"

After that, Harry never mentioned quitting school again.

Their teacher for sixth grade was a pretty young lady by the name of Miss Brockway, who had been hired during the summer. This was her first year of teaching. Peter knew that would be good for Harry, since she would know nothing of the students' backgrounds.

Indeed, she began calling on Harry just as though he were one of the group. And when Avery tried to make trouble for Harry, Miss Brockway scolded him soundly. Peter was pleased.

At recess, however, it was a different story. Avery still held a lot of sway with the boys on the playground. If he said Harry was not to be played with, then that's how it was.

Peter asked Harry to teach him to play mumblety-peg with the jackknife. Peter got pretty good at flipping the knife into the target on the ground, but never as good as Harry.

Peter's job at the livery stable continued for an hour after school each day, and Mr. Kingsbury's business was picking up. Carpenters were busy building an extension on the back of the stable. It would hold several more stalls. After that was finished, Mr. Kingsbury planned to purchase additional horses.

One afternoon, as Peter was spreading fresh straw in the stalls, he watched all the hammering and sawing going on. It made him wonder how Mr. Kingsbury was going to keep up with all the extra work that more horses would create. Suddenly he had an idea. Swinging the last pitchfork full of hay into the stall, he propped the fork against the stall door and went to find his employer. Rags jumped up from where he was lying and trotted along at his heels.

Peter found Mr. Kingsbury in his small cubbyhole office near the front double doors of the livery.

"Mr. Kingsbury, may I talk with you a moment?"

"Sure, Peter. What's on your mind?"

"Sir, are you going to need more help once the new stalls are done?"

"You know of someone?"

Peter nodded. "I sure do. A boy my age. His name is Harry. He could work after school and on Saturdays just like I'm doing."

"Can I count on him? Is he responsible?"

"You can count on him all right," Peter replied. "Up at the lake, he risked his life to save Rags here."

Mr. Kingsbury's dark bushy eyebrows went up. "You don't say. A real hero, huh? Well, bring him around and let's talk."

As Peter walked home for supper that evening, he felt lighter than air. Even though his birthday was getting close and even though he would have to tell Grandpa he didn't have the money, he felt he had something much more important. In this small way, perhaps he could thank Harry for saving Rags's life.

CHAPTER 16
Peter's Birthday

Peter felt a nip in the air as he walked to Grandpa's bank the morning of his twelfth birthday. The fact that he hadn't saved fifteen dollars didn't bother him. But facing Grandpa Enoch bothered him a great deal.

He'd told no one that he hadn't met Grandpa's challenge. Except Carol, of course. Even she didn't know how much he'd spent to help the Dawes family. Nor how often he'd done it. There was no reason to tell. It was a confidence he would never betray.

Since his birthday fell on Friday, Mama had sent a note

to Miss Brockway the previous day saying that Peter would be late for school. He would miss devotions and the story that Miss Brockway read every morning. He should be there in time for arithmetic class, which meant long division, which he hated.

He wished he didn't have to pass the bicycle shop on his way, but there it was, looming in front of him. And there was the royal blue bicycle looking as scrumptious as ever. He paused only a moment before walking on down the busy street. Inside the bank, Josh greeted Peter with a polite smile and ushered him right into Grandpa's office.

"Well, Peter, my boy," Grandpa said after Peter was seated. "I guess you've brought your fifteen dollars and you're ready to go down the street and pick up that new bicycle."

"No, sir."

Grandpa Enoch blinked a couple times and leaned forward in his creaking chair. "Come again?"

"No, sir."

"No, sir, what?"

"No, sir, I've not brought the fifteen dollars."

"Hm, I see." Grandpa rubbed at his bushy white mustache. "I'm sorry to hear that. Mismanaged a little, did you?"

"You could say that."

"I see. Well, let this be a lesson for you of how deceptive money can be. It slips right out of your fingers if you don't watch out."

Peter didn't answer.

"Confound it, Peter!" Grandpa said, hitting the arm of his chair with his fist. "I'd expected better of you."

"Yes, sir." The look of disappointment in Grandpa's

eyes was almost unbearable, but Peter stood his ground. Harry deserved to be protected.

Grandpa sighed. "I'm sorry it has to be this way."

"So am I, sir."

"But a deal is a deal."

"Yes, sir, it is."

"Well, what're you standing around here for? Scoot on off to school or you'll be late." With that, Peter was shooed out of the paneled office.

Father asked him later why he'd come up short with the money, but Peter said he didn't want to talk about it.

Peter had informed Mama he didn't want a big birthday party. He preferred to have Harry and Mattie over and include Uncle Abe and Aunt Elise. If it were small, perhaps Harry wouldn't feel uncomfortable. Also, he didn't want to make Carol feel any worse about her birthday being on Christmas.

Peter received a number of nice gifts. But the nicest of all was a wooden dog that Harry had carved himself. Everyone at the party admired the detail in the carving. Peter could hardly believe how much it looked like Rags.

Mattie had crocheted a nice doily for him. When he opened the package, Mattie said, "It's for your shelf—to put the wooden dog on."

Peter thanked them profusely. He was touched by their thoughtfulness.

By October, the extension on the rear of Kingsbury Livery Stable was completed, the new horses had been purchased, and Harry Dawes was helping out after school.

Peter had had no way of knowing for sure if Harry

would be good with the horses. As it turned out, Harry *was* good with them. He was gentle and patient and willing to learn everything Peter could teach him. With his first pay envelope, Harry purchased a new pinafore for Mattie and groceries for his mama.

Because Harry was working alongside Albert, Albert became more friendly toward Harry at school. "He always seemed like a pretty good Joe to me," Albert said privately to Peter. "I never put much stock in all of Avery's huffing and puffing."

Leaves were falling like golden rain in Fair Oaks as Peter and Harry walked home from work together one evening.

"Did you know your uncle Abe has come visiting us?" Harry said as they walked along.

"I didn't know, but I'm not surprised. That's just like Uncle Abe."

"The first time he came, Father ordered him out of the house."

"He did? Why?"

"Because Mr. Stevenson didn't come for a social call. He came to talk to Papa about the liquor."

"Oh my," Peter said. How could Uncle Abe be so bold? But then, he and Aunt Elise were accustomed to working with drunkards. Peter felt sure they knew best how to handle the situation.

"That night, after your uncle left, Papa became furious and started throwing things. Mattie and I hid in the attic until he calmed down. But good old Abe Stevenson wouldn't give up."

"What do you mean?"

"The next time he came, he brought Mrs. Stevenson

with him. They both talked with Papa. They asked if they could talk to him privately in his study. And you'll never guess what."

"What?"

"He agreed to talk."

"You don't say." Peter was amazed. First the man had ordered Uncle Abe out. Then he agreed to talk.

"Mr. Stevenson told me not to look for any miracles yet. He explained that the power of the liquor is so strong even the most keen-minded of men can be enslaved by it. But he also told me he believes my father truly wants to be free from the power of the drinking."

"That would be wonderful."

"Yeah," Harry agreed. "I've been hoping and praying for so long. Uncle Abe told me that the bindery business is about to go under and that my father feels bad about that. Papa always says he's going to change, but then after a few days, everything is just like before. Maybe this time it'll be different."

"Well, this time, I'm praying with you."

"Thanks, Peter. You're a true friend."

Peter did as he promised. Every night he prayed for the entire Dawes family—especially for Mr. Dawes to be set free.

Often during the cool fall days, Peter would see Heber and Avery taking turns riding Avery's bicycle. Every time he saw the bicycle, it had something new on it—a bell, a leather tool kit, a lantern. Avery had everything.

One evening when Peter arrived home, all the neighbor kids were in the yard playing in great piles of leaves. Even Mark was toddling around. He was all bundled up in his woolen coat and cap. Carol was swinging him around by his arms and letting him land in the soft leaves. Father was getting ready to burn the leaves, but he let the children play as long as they wished.

Instead of going in to change clothes, Peter joined in the happy ruckus. After making a huge leap into the middle of a pile of leaves, he looked up to see Heber standing there.

"May I play?" Heber asked.

Peter almost said, "Where's Avery?" but he held his tongue. Instead, he said, "Come on in." With that he scooped up a huge handful of leaves and threw them at Heber. They raked leaves, piled leaves, jumped in leaves, and threw leaves, being careful all the while to watch out for little Mark. Rags jumped and barked and played right along with them.

When the mothers called them in for supper, Heber said, "See ya, Peter."

"See ya, Hebe."

As they brushed off the leaves and started into the house, Carol said, "Do you think he's done being mad at you?"

Peter shrugged. "I have no idea. But I sure hope so."

CHAPTER 17

Peter's New Bicycle

"Your grandpa wants to see you in the morning," Father said to Peter at the dinner table one evening.

The family was dressed in their good clothes, and each was in place at the table. Mark was now big enough to stay up and eat in his wooden high chair at the table rather than being sent to bed.

Father had finished reading the Scriptures, and Stella had just set the leg of lamb at Father's place. He was carving the slices when he made his announcement.

Peter felt his throat tighten. He looked over at Mama. Mama's tummy was getting rounder and rounder as Christmas drew near. She just shook her head. Evidently she didn't know what the reason for Grandpa's request was.

"May I ask why he wants to see me?" Peter didn't relish another scolding. Or to see Grandpa Enoch slam the arm of the chair with his fist and say, "Confound it."

"I've not been told the reason." Father smiled as he passed each plate to the children in turn. "But you'll come and let me know, won't you?"

From the smile on Father's face, Peter couldn't be sure if he were joshing or not. "Yes, sir, I will."

"I'll telephone the school," Mama said, "to let Miss Brockway know you'll be late."

When a nervous Peter walked into Grandpa's office the next morning, he couldn't believe his eyes. In one of the chairs sat Thomas Dawes. Uncle Abe sat right beside him. As Peter entered, Mr. Dawes stood and came over to shake his hand. Peter's hand was nearly lost in the man's large one.

"Hello, Peter. I've not formally met you, but I've certainly heard a lot about you."

"You have?" Peter looked at Grandpa, who was smiling. What was happening here?

Uncle Abe said, "Come sit down, Peter. We have some good news for you."

As Peter made himself comfortable, Mr. Dawes explained to Peter that he'd asked Jesus to come into his heart and how all his desire for drinking had left. Motioning to Uncle Abe, Mr. Dawes said, "I thank God, Peter, that you brought this man and his wife into my life. I'll never be the same again."

135

The smile that lit Thomas Dawes's face made Peter know it was true.

"I've tried to quit on my own for years," he went on, "but Mrs. Stevenson explained that I needed the power of God working in me. And in order to have the power of God working, I needed Jesus as my Savior. She was right!"

"And," Uncle Abe jumped in, "we've all learned that you supplied the Dawes family with food from time to time. Could that be why you didn't have your fifteen dollars?"

Peter felt his ears burn hot. He hadn't wanted anyone to know. "How did you find out?"

"It wasn't too difficult," Mr. Dawes said with a laugh. "You're not very sneaky. Generous yes, but not very sneaky."

Before Peter could think more about that remark, Grandpa was explaining that Uncle Abe had agreed to personally finance Mr. Dawes's bindery business to bring it out of debt. He would also teach Mr. Dawes good business practices.

That, Peter thought, was just like Uncle Abe. He wondered if Harry was aware of all this good news.

"It's a noble thing you did, Peter," Grandpa continued, "but why didn't you tell me why you didn't have the money?"

"I promised not to tell anyone," Peter replied.

"Even if it meant not receiving the bicycle for your birthday?"

Peter nodded. "Yes, sir. Even if it meant that."

"Peter Morgan," Grandpa said, hitting the arm of his chair with his fist, "you've more than earned your bicycle! You've more than proven yourself to me."

Peter could hardly believe what he was hearing.

"Abe is going to go to Holmgren's with you now,"

Grandpa said, "and get that bicycle. You can ride it on to school."

"Thank you, sir. I'll bring what money I have to you just as soon as I can."

Grandpa waved his hand. "No, no. You keep your money. I don't want your money. I only wanted to test your mettle!"

Uncle Abe stood. "Come on, Peter. Let's go get that bicycle."

Peter started to go, then turned to Grandpa. "Sir. I'd like to say something."

"Yes?"

"You said you were proud of me for helping Mr. Dawes. But sir, this is the kind of work Aunt Elise does every day down at the mission. She and Uncle Abe are the ones we should thank. If it weren't for them, none of this miracle might ever have happened."

"The boy's right," Mr. Dawes said. "His aunt is an incredible lady. She and her co-workers at the mission are angels of mercy."

Grandpa cleared his throat and shuffled a few papers on his desk. Perhaps he was remembering all the unkind things he'd said about Aunt Elise and her work. "I hear what you're saying, Peter," Grandpa said softly. "Let's just say I'll, uh, I'll take the matter under advisement."

Before leaving the bank, Peter ran to Father's office to share with him the wonderful news. From the look on Father's face, Peter guessed Father already knew the details.

At the bicycle shop, Mr. Holmgren took the royal blue bicycle out of the window and pumped air into the tires to make them fat and firm. Uncle Abe wrote out the check and handed it to the man, and Peter rolled the vehicle out the front door.

There was snow on the streets, but most of the sidewalks were clear. Peter would have ridden the bicycle if the snow had been knee-deep.

"You're a fine young man, Peter. We're all proud of you."

"Thank you, Uncle Abe. Thank you very much." Then right there on the street, Peter gave his uncle a hug—holding the handlebars with one hand, of course.

The other students were out at recess when Peter arrived. What fun it was to see the shock on Avery's face when Peter came riding his blue bicycle right onto the school grounds! And how wonderful it was to tell Harry that his father's business was being saved!

CHAPTER 18
Holly for Christmas

Christmas that year was extra special. On Christmas Eve, both Saint Nicholas and another person visited the Morgan home. When the Morgan children awoke, they discovered they had a new baby sister. Father announced that her name was Holly.

Mother had been staying in the downstairs guest room prior to the baby's arrival. The children were allowed to tip-toe in and see their new sister. Then Father had them sit on the floor as he read to them the Christmas story from the book of Luke.

Since Mother had to stay in bed, they agreed to bring all their gifts into her room and open them.

Peter received a tool kit for his bicycle and a bell for the handlebars. Carol and Allyson were both thrilled with pairs of roller skates. Mark was fascinated with his wind-up toys.

Once all the gifts were opened, Peter went out into the hall and brought in a large box for Carol. On top were the words, "Happy Birthday."

"What could this be?" she asked.

"Open it and see," Peter said, hardly able to contain himself.

She opened the box only to find layers and layers of tissue paper. Throwing paper every which way, she finally discovered an envelope at the very bottom. She studied it, turning it over and over in her hands.

"Open it, open it," Allyson said, clapping her hands with glee.

Tearing the envelope open, Carol pulled out a letter.

"Read it out loud," Peter said. Carol did as he asked:

Dear Carol,

Beginning in 1897, the Morgan family agrees to celebrate the birthday of Carol Morgan on her 'half-birthday' of June 25th. We will celebrate said half-birthday for every succeeding year until such time that Carol agrees to return the celebration to Christmas Day.

The letter was signed by every member of the family—

even a scribble by Mark. And at the very bottom of the page was a tiny fingerprint from Baby Holly.

Carol looked around at her family, her eyes brimming with bright tears. "Thank you all. Thank you so much. This is my best birthday-Christmas gift ever!"

"It was all Peter's idea," Mama said.

Suddenly Carol was hugging Peter's neck right in front of the whole family. After hugging each person, she went to the baby and kissed her tiny soft cheek. "What about Holly?" Carol asked. "She's going to have the same dilemma."

But Father answered, "Every person is different, Carol. Who knows? Perhaps Baby Holly will enjoy having her birthday on Christmas."

At that moment, Holly set up a wail just as though she were voicing her opinion right then, which made them all laugh.

Following the Christmas services at church, the Morgans gathered at Grandpa Enoch's house for Christmas dinner. Mama, of course, stayed home with the baby.

To their great surprise, Grandma Tina had invited the Dawes family to come to dinner as well. Peter sat right next to Harry at dinner and Carol was beside Mattie.

As they ate, Harry leaned over to Peter and whispered, "This is the best Christmas our family ever had. And guess what?"

"What?" Peter asked.

Harry beamed a wide smile. "Papa promised me I may have my own bicycle for my birthday in March!"

"Great! Then we can go riding everywhere together!"

After a wonderful dinner, there were yet more gifts to

open under Grandpa's tree. Peter couldn't remember ever being so happy.

Mrs. Dawes kept gazing adoringly at Mr. Dawes. And Mr. Dawes kept holding his wife's hand. At one point the shy, quiet Mrs. Dawes thanked the group for all their kindness to her. Then she said, "God has given me back my husband. That's the best Christmas gift one could ever have."

Later that afternoon, there was a knock at the door. Grandpa's butler said it was for Peter. Peter went to the door to find Avery and Heber standing there, red-faced from the cold.

"Hello, Peter," Avery said. "Hebe and me want to know if you and Harry can play. We have a snow fort started in the vacant lot. We sure could use some help."

"And I got a toboggan for Christmas," Heber added. "It's big enough for four."

Peter turned around and hollered, "Harry, come here!" He'd never hollered in Grandpa's house before, but no one scolded him.

Harry came rushing through the foyer. "What is it?"

Peter pointed to Heber and Avery. "They want to know if we can play snow fort and go tobogganing with them."

"You bet!" Harry said. "Let's get our coats."

"Oh, one thing," Avery said. "Harry, I have something for you." He held out a mitten-covered hand.

Harry held out his hand, and into it Avery dropped a brass key. "Merry Christmas."

"Thank you, Avery," Harry said. There was a little catch in his voice.

"Here's your key back, Peter," Avery said.

Peter reached out his hand and felt the cold brass key in

his palm. It was still strung on the piece of dirty string he'd worn for so many months.

"Hurry," Heber said. "Get your coats. Last one to the fort is as rotten as Dangerous Dan."

Harry and Peter pulled on their coats, caps, and gloves and raced out into the deep snow on the heels of Avery and Heber.

"Hurrah for the Shady Vinewood Club," Peter shouted.

"Hurrah for the Shady Vinewood Club," Harry echoed as he sped past.

"Goodness, how that boy can run," Peter said between breaths.

"Even with shoes on," Avery replied, laughing.

Harry passed them all and beat them to the vacant lot by a mile—whooping every step of the way!

There's More!

The American Adventure continues with *The New Citizen*. Mark Morgan and his cousin Maureen O'Callaghan Stevenson need to solve a mystery. Priceless art objects in Old Lady Figg's mansion are disappearing. The police think Mrs. Figg is crazy, so they don't take her reports seriously. But Mark and Maureen are beginning to believe the elderly widow is telling the truth. Who would do such a thing? And why?

Then tragedy strikes Mark's family. How can Maureen and Mrs. Figg help Mark with his troubles? And will the mystery at Figg mansion be solved before something terrible happens to Mrs. Figg?